EVA CHASE

FALSE AUGURY

TRAITOR OF VILLAINS

False Augury

Book 2 in the Traitor of Villains series

First Digital Edition, 2020

Copyright © 2021 Eva Chase

Cover design: Christian Bentulan, Covers by Christian

Ebook ISBN: 978-1-989096-89-5

Paperback ISBN: 978-1-990338-05-2

 Created with Vellum

CHAPTER ONE

Cressida

The suffocating sense that something was horribly *wrong* wrapped around me before I'd even fully emerged from sleep. That tension tainted my first impressions as my awareness came back to me. I was lying down—on a hard, smooth surface. Something pressed against my wrists. A fog filled my head, muddling my thoughts.

I rubbed my eyes and opened them. Only dim light streaked into the space from a single window near the ceiling, too small for me to make out anything beyond it from my present position. I was lying a couple of feet from a plain beige wall on a tiled floor. Narrow metal bands encircled my wrists tightly, with a chain connecting them to each other and to a thick ring embedded in the wall.

What the fuck?

I jerked into full alertness, the fog rolling back with

the force of a surge of panic. I shoved myself upright, yanking at the cuffs instinctively, a casting word rising up my throat. But even as it tumbled off my mouth, I recognized the design of the cuffs. No magic stirred inside me with the word. Where normally my stores of collected fear energy formed a mild tingling between my ribs, now my chest felt vacant.

A voice rasped behind me. "They're the warded cuffs like the blacksuits use. No way to use our magic while they're on us."

With a hitch of my pulse, I whipped around as quickly as the chain allowed. There was a whole lot more of the room—about twenty feet of the same beige walls and tiled floor, with more ominous rings mounted at intervals along that wall. Chained to the farthest one, directly across from me, sat Noah Ashgrave.

He was leaning against the wall with his legs loosely drawn up in front of him and his hands resting on his knees, linked by the same kind of cuffs and chain as mine were. His black hair fell messily across his forehead and along his cheeks, unbound from its usual short ponytail, and a shadow had crossed his eyes, which were normally so bright with energy and amusement. His mouth slanted at an uncertain angle.

Seeing him jolted me back to my last memories before this room—to being shoved into the back of the Achelings' sedan and finding him sprawled unconscious on the seat. And then… and then a blast of magic had blacked out my mind.

My stomach knotted. The fearmancer families we'd

been investigating, lower level ones among the group who called themselves "reapers" and were looking to unseat the new barons, must have realized I wasn't really coming back into the fold. Maybe because they'd discovered Noah, one of the barons-to-be and younger brother to a baron who'd already claimed the title, had followed me to Portland. Or maybe that had come afterward. Had I slipped up somewhere while I'd been playing the role of contrite daughter and co-conspirator?

I was still wearing the sleek knee-length dress I'd put on for my next meeting with the reapers, but my shoes had gotten lost along the way, my feet bare against the cool tiles. My purse—and my phone and everything else I'd been carrying—was long gone.

Where the hell had they brought us to? Were we still in Portland? In Maine?

More importantly, what were they planning on doing with us now that I'd proven myself a traitor to their cause twice over?

"Are you okay?" I asked.

Obviously none of this was okay in a general sense, but Noah took the question in the spirit I intended it. His mouth shifted into a smile that looked uncomfortably close to a grimace. He cleared his throat and gave the collar of his casual button-up a quick tug. His voice came out a little smoother this time. "I've felt better, that's for sure, but they don't seem to have hurt me at all. You?"

He studied me, his gaze intense enough to send a flicker of warmth through my body, followed by a lump that clogged in my throat. I'd only just started to realize how much my safety and happiness meant to the guy sitting across from me. He'd been taking care of me with little kindnesses for months while I'd assumed he was only making sure I wasn't *really* a reaper spy. It was probably killing him more that I'd ended up in chains than that he had.

But it was my fault that *he* was here. We could have ended the operation already, gone back to the security of Bloodstone Academy after we'd uncovered the plans the Portland reapers were making. Instead, I'd decided I just had to play hero and dive in even farther, in the hopes of getting some dirt on the more prominent reaper families and *their* schemes…

I should have known by now that heroics weren't my forte.

I adjusted my position, checking for subtle pains, but other than some lingering stiffness from lying on the hard floor, I seemed to be fine. "Same. What happened? I came down to the car like I was meant to, and they already had you… I didn't have a chance to try to fight back."

Noah's expression was definitely a grimace now. "Neither did I. I'm not even sure how they did it. I must have gotten careless and not checked my protections on the room closely enough. I was just sitting on the bed watching TV when all of a sudden I got so tired… I think they managed to cast the spell from one of the neighboring rooms. And after I was out, they must have broken into the room and grabbed me. Next thing I knew, I was waking up in here."

"Has anyone come—do you know who's taken us?"

Wilhelm and Flora Acheling were involved, presumably, since it'd been one of their staff who'd opened the car door for me, but had they been acting alone or with the other Portland reaper families?

Noah shook his head. "I'd estimate I only came to ten minutes before you did. But maybe they'll come by soon now that we're both up."

He made a subtle gesture toward the ceiling with a widening of his eyes, and I caught his drift immediately. Chances were we were being watched and recorded, probably with cameras hidden by illusion magic we couldn't dispel while we had these cuffs on. That was why they'd have stuck us in here together: to give us a chance to spill something they could use against us or the barons —our friends and, in Noah's case, family—back home.

I swallowed thickly. How much could I safely say? I didn't want to make the horrible situation we'd found ourselves in even worse.

"I guess we'll just have to wait and see, then," I said, my mind whipping through various possibilities. If Noah had been caught so off-guard, there was no way he'd have had a chance to alert the barons. How long would it take before Rory and the rest realized our mission had been compromised and that we were in trouble? I itched to ask Noah how often they'd expected him to check in, but that definitely wasn't the kind of information I wanted our captors overhearing.

Even if the barons had already figured out that something had happened to us, how likely was it that they'd be able to find us? Tracking beacon spells were notoriously difficult both to cast and maintain—to work properly, they had to continue giving off energy constantly, and a lot if they were going to have any range. We hadn't cast anything like that on ourselves during the mission because it'd have been impossible to make one powerful enough to reach across multiple state lines anyway. And it wasn't as if we could reach out magically now.

Noah was still watching me, maybe guessing at the direction my thoughts had taken. His face had gotten even more serious. When I looked at him again, the regret in his eyes sent another jab of guilt through my gut.

"I'm sorry," he said.

"It's not your fault. None of this is your fault."

"If I'd taken better precautions—"

"We don't know how they found out about you," I reminded him. "Anyway, it doesn't matter now. We're here —all we can focus on is what happens next."

It *did* matter to me—that guilt wasn't going away anytime soon—but I didn't want him dwelling on it when he shouldn't have to.

The lock on the door clicked. With a squeak of its hinges, a stony-faced man I'd never seen before appeared in the doorway. He walked over to me without so much as a glance at Noah. "Miss Warbury, your presence is required upstairs."

Whoever this prison belonged to, they were awfully polite to their captives. I scooted back against the wall instinctively. "Who are you? Why am I here?"

"I'm sure my employers will go over all of that with

you," he said in the same nonchalant tone, as if I'd come here for a job interview and not in chains. A prickling sensation wound through my abdomen.

Even the patriarchs of the Portland families hadn't carried themselves with this much cool disinterest. No, this dude's attitude reminded me unnervingly of the staff in my own family's house and those they'd socialized with.

I'd bet good money that we were dealing with a much higher level of the reaper hierarchy now. Possibly its peak.

Considering the guy had about half a foot on me and full use of his magic, I didn't see that putting up a fight was likely to get me anywhere. Gritting my teeth, I raised my hands. With a brief word, the man unlatched the length of chain that had connected me to the wall. With my wrists still cuffed and bound together, I scrambled to my feet.

Without another word, the guy ushered me out of the room. I shot a quick glance Noah's way in an attempt at reassurance, but I had no idea how well it worked. I'd already known we were in deep shit. It might have just graduated from over our heads to a bottomless pit.

We headed down a bland hallway and up a flight of tiled steps to what I guessed was the building's ground level. My first glimpse of a broad floor-to-ceiling window in the room we were approaching confirmed that. Beyond a circular driveway with several cars parked along its arc, thick forest filled the view as far as I could see. The vibrant hardwood floors and deep green walls added to the wilderness chalet impression.

This must be one of the isolated country homes that

fearmancers in my parents' circle liked to keep—somewhere well off the beaten track, away from nonmagical Nary eyes, where they could do whatever they liked without worrying about random passersby. From the poshness of the main floor, I'd estimate they were wealthy enough to own at least a hundred acres of the land around here.

We were well and truly beyond the reach of civilization.

The sun beaming high above the treetops suggested it was already midday. The spell had knocked me out good. I squinted at the driveway, scanning for any detail that might be useful. Then my escort nudged me through the doorway all the way into the room ahead, and all thought of the scene *outside* fled my mind with a flood of cold.

Several figures were gathered in front of me, sitting on the plump leather furniture or standing around it, watching my arrival. Off to one side hovered Wilhelm and Flora Acheling, as well as Octavian Haythorpe... and Emeric Riplowe, my other ally in my investigations. Seated on a loveseat at a studied distance from them were a couple with perfectly tailored clothes who I didn't recognize at all. Two men I vaguely remembered from my parents' social circle were poised on and beside a nearby armchair.

Finally, lounging with a whole sofa to himself and a steely glint in his dark eyes, there was my father.

My throat closed up. I hadn't seen either of my parents since I'd thrown my lot in with Rory Bloodstone and the scions during the war with the old barons. They'd made their displeasure with me blatantly known, though. Right now I could practically see Dad imagining how he'd flay me open.

I jerked my gaze away, and it landed back on Emeric. He was staring at me too, with a crooked frown. He'd been pretending to work with the Portland reapers while he actually helped me investigate their schemes. Had they found out about his duplicity and brought him here as a captive too?

But although the Achelings and Octavian had positioned themselves as if they didn't want it to appear that they included Emeric as a real companion, no cuffs restrained his wrists—the one of flesh or the titanium one of his prosthetic hand and forearm, hidden beneath his usual leather gloves. His cinnamon brown hair was in its usual tousled state but not overly messy, and his fitted tee showed no sign of being slept in like the wrinkles that'd formed in my dress. He looked uncomfortable but not trapped.

A quiver of hope passed through my chest. He must be keeping up his ruse—he'd heard what had happened to Noah and me and managed to score an invite to this… get-together. Maybe he'd find a way to get us out of it.

He'd called me right before the Achelings' car came. The conversation had been so short and unwanted, I'd almost forgotten. He'd apologized for running off on me like I disgusted him when we'd been a few pieces of clothes short of having sex and… and he'd said we needed to talk.

He'd sounded urgent about it. Had he already suspected something was going wrong?

As annoyed as I'd been with him, it seemed I should have listened.

I suppressed any sign that I was happy to see him. I couldn't let our audience know that we'd been working together to undermine the reapers. Instead, I looked at the couple from the loveseat, who'd just stood up. Two bucks said this was their chalet.

"Well, here is Cressida Warbury," the woman said, stalking in a slow circle around me with a predatory grace and a haughtily raised chin. "What will we do with you?"

My nerves were so frazzled I lost control over my tongue. "I don't know. You're the ones who brought me here—shouldn't you have figured that out already?"

Her husband snorted. "Still some spirit in her. You didn't manage to break that." He tossed a careless glance toward the Portland group and rocked on his heels, his head cocked, eyeing me. "You were an unexpected gift, my dear. We're simply deciding whether you're worth much of a reward."

Wilhelm spoke up, his voice both hurried and deferential. "The reward isn't just *her*. You've gotten our records of all the humiliations we put her through, the way we forced her to smear the imposter barons. She deserved to be punished, and we saw that through on your behalf." His gaze flicked to where my father was sitting at the edge of my vision.

Wait, what? They... punished me? My arms stiffened as my mind reeled with that new perspective. Yeah, I'd ended up doing some embarrassing things to convince them I was really on their side... I'd worn that ridiculous costume at a party, I'd kissed one asshole's freaking *shoes*. But that—that had all been part of the role I was playing.

Had they never really meant to accept my apologies and repentance? They'd just been stringing me along, wringing all the humiliation they could out of the situation?

Dad stirred for the first time, leaning forward with his elbow still slung casually over the arm of the sofa. He made a faint tsking sound that sent the hairs on the back of my neck on end in an instant. "You had no idea they brought you in for their own purposes, did you? These plebs played you like a fiddle, and you fell for it. Even after you bought into the rhetoric of those pathetic excuses for barons, I'd have hoped for a little better from the girl I raised."

Brought me *in* for their own purposes? But the Achelings hadn't brought me to Portland. I'd only come because Emeric... because Emeric had said there was some awful plan against the barons that we needed to stop...

My stomach was already plummeting when Flora spoke up, jabbing Emeric's arm with her finger. There was a curtness to her normally breezy voice. "Don't listen if this one tries to tell you he came up with the whole plot on his own. We all discussed it together. That family of his barely has their act together. We only kept him involved because he was our best shot at getting into the university to reach her."

No. She couldn't be saying—

But the pieces clicked into place all too neatly, leaving me dizzied.

The entire thing had been a set-up from the start. There hadn't really been any conspiracy to uncover. Emeric had made it up to remove me from the barons' protection, to give his reaper *friends* an excuse to run me through their paces.

The urge to vomit rolled over me. Emeric didn't say anything at all, his gaze darting away when I looked at him again.

Oblivious to my inner turmoil, the reapers kept talking as if they were haggling over a used car.

"It doesn't matter who was more or less responsible for your arrangements if she isn't worth anything to us," the predatory woman said. "As amusing as your videos and photographs might be, that's all done now. Who can say how much the imposter barons will even care about one middling mage with a history among their enemies? The boy will make a much better bargaining chip."

"You wouldn't have gotten him if we hadn't reeled her in," Octavian pointed out in his usual peevish way.

"And you will be appropriately compensated." Her husband gave the other man a dour look. "But perhaps we should have you take this one back with you. Hardly worth the hassle."

Octavian's gaunt cheeks flushed red.

Wilhelm gave a short cough, drawing his burly form a little more stoutly straight. "We've gathered that she's become very close with the Bloodstone girl in particular. Isn't the supposed Baron Bloodstone the worst thorn in your side? The imposter barons clearly value Cressida's skills, or they wouldn't have trusted her to carry out this 'mission' for them."

"Perhaps we will find some use for her," my father said with the same cold disdain as before. "It will take some thinking—and some discussion I expect neither she nor you should be privy to."

The man who escorted me upstairs grasped my arm. My legs balked instinctively, but what the hell could I say? My mind was still spinning, all the events of the past few weeks upended and jumbled into a horrifying mess.

I'd trusted Emeric, confided in him, and he'd used me in a way a hundred times worse than I could ever have suspected. And now Noah and I were imprisoned here, miles upon miles distant from anyone who wasn't looking to carve us up for spare parts, not a single soul on our side.

My innards had turned to ice. No doubt every reaper in the room had caught at least a taste of that fear. The best I could do was set my expression into a rigid mask to keep some tiny appearance of dignity and let their underling lead me away before my rising sense of hopelessness completely wrenched me apart.

CHAPTER TWO

Emeric

Octavian stalked from one end of the sitting room to the other, his breaths coming out in sharp little huffs. "Ridiculous. We bring them prize upon prize, and they won't even give us a seat in the discussion."

Flora shot him a disdainful look from the armchair she was perched on and fluffed her ruby-red hair. "They didn't accumulate all the power they have by letting mages into their confidence willy-nilly. We just have to continue playing our cards right."

"Or perhaps this upstart led us up the wrong tree to begin with," Wilhelm muttered, narrowing his eyes at me.

I offered him a thin smile even as my gut twisted at the reminder that this entire scheme *had* essentially been my idea—though of course these pricks would only give me that credit when they were looking for someone to blame, not praise. My plan to win myself more respect among the Portland sect of reaper families had worked about as well as the overall plan to win ourselves the favor of the highest of the reapers. After all I'd done to get them here, they still looked at me as if I were a stray mutt scratching at their door.

"We're here, aren't we?" I took a gulp from the glass of wine I was clutching a little too tightly, letting the sour tang and the faint buzz that followed it smooth out the edge that was creeping into my voice. "If you had some other plan for getting an invitation into a home like this, you were welcome to carry it out without me."

Where would I be if they had? It was hard to imagine. Maybe I wouldn't have been much happier. But the image of Cressida's pretty, pale face turning completely white as she understood what I'd done lingered behind my eyes, making the wine churn queasily inside me.

I set down the glass on the cedar buffet and turned toward the window so the others couldn't see my expression. The shadowed forest glowered back at me.

I'd thought this was what I wanted. A few months ago, dropping Shauna off at the university, I'd seen Cressida Warbury strutting across the lawn, her head high and her expression lofty, as if she couldn't be prouder of the life she'd made for herself. As if, as long as she got everything *she* wanted, she didn't give a crap what the rest of us might have been through while she turned her back on her family and her community. What the rest of us had lost.

My stomach listed again, and the fingers on my titanium hand flexed automatically, the magic embedded in it sending tingles of sensation through my nerves. That section of arm wasn't even the worst of my losses.

But I'd been wrong about Cressida. She'd lost things too—there were things it sounded like she'd never even *had* that I'd taken for granted… When I thought of her blue-gray eyes gazing up at me from her bed, her voice so raw as she'd told me she'd only been fighting for her own survival…

I closed my own eyes against the image. It'd taken me too long to decide how I felt about her confession. To break through all the layers of resentment and anger I'd built up over the past two years and really consider at what I was doing. To look properly at everything she'd shown me since I'd met her. And then by the time I'd found out that the Achelings were moving forward with the rest of the plot already, it'd been too late to warn her.

Well, that wasn't totally true. It might not have been too late if I hadn't stormed off the way I had after her confession, so she'd have been willing to listen to me in the brief window I'd gotten on the phone.

So, yes, this had all been my idea, the consequences were pretty much entirely my fault, and I was getting no satisfaction from that knowledge.

"*You* don't seem all that pleased with the outcome so far, Riplowe," Octavian snarked at my back. "Why should I be?"

As I turned around, I forced another smile onto my face. I had to keep up appearances while I was here, while I was figuring out what the hell to do next. Had to pretend I was just as committed as I'd always been. None of them appeared to suspect that I'd nearly destroyed their plans at the last minute.

As long as I was here, I might find a chance to get Cressida out of this after all. That was the least I owed her.

If the Kingsleys and their friends didn't subject her to some even more horrible fate first. The way Cressida's own father had eyed her, as if he were picturing slitting her throat… A shiver ran through me at the memory.

"I *would* like to see that they fully appreciate how we've contributed," I said. "But we have made it pretty far from Portland. I think we should all try to be patient."

Flora hummed to herself. "*I* think I wouldn't take advice from a crippled cast-off." She turned to her husband. "We'll see that they recognize us as we deserve. I'm not leaving here without an invitation to join in their efforts against the new barons."

Something in me bristled at her insult, but over the past two years, I'd gotten very good at hiding my feelings. The fact that Cressida hadn't suspected my true intentions even after I'd shoved her away proved that.

At this point, nothing this bunch said could really get to me. I'd heard it all.

No, I didn't care what they were saying. I'd really like to know what the higher families were deciding right now.

"It doesn't seem as if they're in any hurry to bring us into the discussion at the moment," I said, carefully even. "I'll be in my room if there's any news."

With false nonchalance, I ambled out of the room the Kingsleys' had given for our daytime use and down the hall. This place's owners were rich enough that their "cottage" home had guestrooms to spare, even for guests they hadn't anticipated and didn't particularly want. But I walked right past those doors, deeper into the building.

Where were the higher reapers having their chat? If I could manage to listen in on at least a bit of it, get some sense of their plans, I'd have a better idea of how much time I had to work with and what obstacles I needed to navigate around.

I peered around a corner just as one of the staff emerged from a room partway down, carrying a tray of empty glasses. Ah ha. I pulled back until the woman had disappeared from view and then eased down the hall, studying the door.

I wasn't likely to get away with pressing my ear up to the crack here in the middle of the hall. But my physicality skills could help me with a subtler strategy. I just needed to get into one of the neighboring rooms…

The door to the left of the meeting room balked at my twist of the knob, but the one on the right opened into a small library. While built-in shelves lined most of the walls, there was a bare stretch forming an alcove for a chaise lounge partway along the one I needed. I knelt on the silk cushion and leaned close to the plaster surface.

With a murmured casting word, I dug away at the plaster until only a thin layer remained between me and the neighboring room. When I tipped even closer to that spot, voices filtered through to my straining ear.

"—the opportunity to damage these imposters from the inside. We'd just have to be careful how we time the detonation for maximum impact."

"I still say it's relying quite a lot on unstable factors. There are so many ways it could go wrong, and the possibility of detection…"

"I believe the new strategy we've perfected will help with the latter concern."

A chuckle rang out. "Exactly. And like Baldric said, one looks a gift horse too closely in the mouth."

I couldn't make out the voices clearly enough to tell who was speaking, but their meaning was clear enough. They had some kind of explosive weapon they were hoping to strike at the new barons with. Something they thought they could disguise as a gift? It didn't sound as if that had anything to do with their captives, though. Had they already finished discussing what they were going to do with Cressida and the Ashgrave scion?

There were a few lower murmurs I didn't catch, followed by one of the louder voices. "Yes, we'd need to determine the most ideal trigger. What stimuli are likely to be present at the ideal time… and whether to go for a gradual escalation or a real blast."

"What about the—"

A creak of the floor just outside the library made me jerk back. At the click of the knob turning, I tossed my casting word at the wall as hastily as I could. The plaster flew back into place, maybe slightly more dimpled than it'd been before, and I managed to leap to my feet and set my hand on one of the shelves before the door had swung all the way open.

The skin-headed man who'd brought Cressida up from

the basement peered in at me. "What are *you* doing in here?" he said in a voice that was almost a growl.

I held up my hands, plastering on the most innocent expression I could summon. "My apologies. I couldn't help poking around a little, thought I might borrow a book to pass the time. I'd be sure to return it."

"You shouldn't be in here at all." He motioned me out with no sympathy at all for my supposed boredom. His gaze dropped to my prosthetic arm, obviously aware of what it was even though I had my gloves on, and his lips curled with a hint of a sneer. "Stick to the rooms you've been given unless you're called on, or I'll happily toss you into the wilds out there with only what you've got on your back."

So much for hospitality. If this was the attitude the Kingsleys' employees had, I hated to think how the bosses treated anyone they had a beef with.

What fate had they chosen for Cressida? I wouldn't put it past them to simply kill her in some horrible way just to send a message about the consequences of turning against the reapers.

As I stepped into the hall, the nausea that came with that thought propelled more words from my throat. "Maybe I could be a little more useful to your employers while I'm here. You must need meals prepared and brought down to the prisoners."

The lights overhead flickered, and the man scowled at them before returning his gaze to me. Anabel Kingsley had made a brief mention when the same thing had happened last night that their private generator out here had become a bit erratic. Now, I filed that fact away for later.

"We'll see," the man said, practically shoving me back toward my rooms, but his voice had softened a bit as if he was considering my suggestion. I strode off with an only slightly lighter heart.

I had to get to Cressida somehow. I'd set this disaster into motion, and it was up to me to fix it before the other families decided to blast *her* away.

CHAPTER THREE

Cressida

After being paraded in front of the reapers upstairs, I had plenty of time to stew over what I'd learned from them. Noah had clearly noted my troubled mood the moment I'd been marched back into the room, but I wasn't sure how much I should say with who knew how many hostile eyes watching our every move.

I wasn't even totally sure yet what I *had* learned. Getting me to Portland had been just part of a larger scheme? Somehow Emeric had tricked the barons into believing his story and that he was honestly on our side?

Well, I guessed that aspect wasn't totally unbelievable. I'd gone through some exercises with Rory and the others to make sure I'd be able to keep up my own pretenses around the reapers even if they used insight or persuasion spells. No doubt Emeric had been preparing for their probing for quite a while.

And then he'd cozied up to me, pretended we were some kind of kindred spirits shedding our questionable pasts, encouraged me to open up, romanced me with supposed tenderness…

What had his end game been *there*? Just to get us to the point of nearly falling into bed together and then crushing me with his rejection? I didn't see how that fit into the reapers' overall plan, but clearly there was a lot I hadn't seen in general about Emeric.

My hands clenched in my lap. Then an even more chilling thought occurred to me. Rory had been a good friend to me—better than I probably deserved—but the other barons and everyone else at Blood U couldn't have been quite as sure of my loyalties considering how aggressively my family had worked against the new fearmancer rulers. What if the reapers made it out as if I'd been in on their plan myself? They could pretend it'd all been a scheme to capture one of the scions that Emeric and I had colluded on…

And if they killed me, I wouldn't get a chance to speak up in my defense. That would be my final legacy.

My gaze darted across the room to Noah, who glanced at me when he noticed my attention on him. He'd been waiting patiently for me to decide what I felt comfortable saying to him, not pushing at all. He was *always* so patient with me, with all the angst I'd dumped in his lap over the past few weeks.

He'd never think I'd been working against him and the other heirs all this time, would he?

The jab of distress that came with that question didn't

matter. How I felt about this situation didn't matter at all. I had to tell him at least enough to prepare him before the reapers dragged him upstairs to do who knew what to him.

It couldn't hurt us for them to hear me repeat what they'd all seen me take in upstairs, right? They'd already been able to tell I hadn't known before.

"It was a set-up," I said. My voice came out croaky— the bastards hadn't even offered us a drink since we'd come to. I swallowed thickly to clear my throat.

Noah frowned. His eyes flicked toward the ceiling, seeking out the possible recording devices, before returning to me. "What do you mean?"

"Coming to Portland to investigate the plot against the barons. Investigating the local reaper families, working to get into their good graces. They meant for us to come. And Emeric was in on it the whole time."

Saying it out loud made my chest tighten all over again. I pushed myself onward. "I think they must have made up the whole thing about hacking into the security systems. They just wanted to get me away from Blood U's protections, embarrass me any way they could, and then offer me up to the higher-level reapers like a present."

Noah's jaw had gone slack. He snapped his mouth shut, staring at me. "But—the barons hashed it all out. No way would Declan have agreed if Emeric's story hadn't seemed totally above board."

His older brother was definitely the biggest advocate for caution among the new barons. I shrugged weakly. "They obviously planned it well. We thought I was going to play the reapers, but it was the other way around the whole time."

The admission exhausted me, even though I'd been in a magically-induced slumber for the better part of the last twenty-four hours. I tipped my head back against the wall, closing my eyes against a sudden prickle of tears. I'd been so stupid, thinking I could stand up for the barons—*fight* for them, like Rory had supported me all this time.

Noah, with his frequently annoying gift for regular insight, must have picked up on my line of thinking with no magic necessary. "It's not your fault."

I opened my eyes again but just gazed at the bland beige ceiling. "I was the one on the front lines, dealing with the reaper families and Emeric. I'm sure there were signs I didn't pick up on but should have."

"If they managed to come up with a solid enough plan to convince not just my brother but Rory and Malcolm and the others—of course they were prepared to handle us once we were here."

"Well, then it was my fault for insisting we stay on longer and try to dig up even more dirt on them. Maybe if we'd left after we got—"

I cut myself off, remembering that as far as we knew, I'd been able to cover up my covert activities in Wilhelm Acheling's office. I might actually have passed on something useful from his computer to the barons, even if not about the plans we'd assumed they were making. I'd come up with that tactic all on my own—Emeric hadn't even known I was going to do it. Wilhelm must have realized I'd been up to *something* when he'd caught me there, but he hadn't necessarily figured out just how much data I'd been able to transmit.

If I'd managed to give our side at least a little bit of an edge, I didn't want the reapers finding out about it.

"—after we thought we had everything we needed," I finished awkwardly. "Maybe if we'd left then instead of me trying to stay on and go after them more…"

"We can't know that," Noah said. "And you were only trying to help as much as you could. Don't beat yourself up over that decision. We're here now—no way of knowing how it might have gone differently."

"Yeah." I couldn't put much conviction into my agreement. "They're talking about using you for some kind of leverage against the barons. As a hostage, I guess."

"I figured." His mouth formed a crooked smile. "Good thing it wasn't someone more valuable who came along, huh?"

I resisted the urge to scoff. Maybe he was trying to convince anyone watching that he wouldn't be worth all that much to the barons back home. I couldn't believe he wouldn't know that Declan would be desperate to get him out of the reapers' hands, and the others would be pretty worked up about his capture too. I simply raised my eyebrows slightly and said, "Right," in a voice that held just a trace of sarcasm.

We lapsed into a brief silence broken by the click of the lock. As the door swung open, I tensed, expecting it to be the same jerk who'd ushered me upstairs coming to collect Noah for the reapers' inspection.

Emeric stepped into the room carrying a tray. At the

sight of his impassive face, my spine went even more rigid. My teeth set on edge. The shame and shock that'd gripped me when I'd first found out about his deception had fermented into an acidic burn of anger that now surged into my chest.

Emeric didn't even look at me. He carried the tray over to Noah, keeping a careful distance just beyond the reach of the chain, and set a bottle of water and a plate with a sandwich where the scion would just be able to reach it.

In the hall beyond, the overhead lights stuttered. Emeric turned toward me, his head bowed low, his gaze focused somewhere in the vicinity of my bare feet. He walked over and crouched down to repeat the same process on my side of the room.

I held my tongue even as the burning sensation crept up my throat. *I* wasn't going to be the first one to speak.

As Emeric set my bottle of water down with a harder *thump* than he'd given the other one, his lips moved with a casting word so quiet the noise of the bottle hitting the floor covered it. At the same moment, the lights outside sputtered—and went completely out. The only illumination left was the thin streak of daylight that shone through the little window high above our heads.

Emeric's head snapped up so his gaze could meet my accusing stare. In that instant, so much anguish showed in his mist-green eyes that my fury twisted into something more painful.

"I'm sorry," he said, quick and hushed. "I don't have time to explain everything, but I'm going to do everything I can to get you out of here."

Understanding hit me. He must have knocked the power out with his spell—whatever cameras were in this room wouldn't be recording us right now. But still—

My voice came out sharp enough to cut. "How do you expect me to believe anything you say after what I just found out?" This could be yet another trick to try to re-earn my trust for who knew what ends. How pathetic did the reapers think I was?

Emeric's square jaw twitched with a subtle tick. I'd seen it before—whenever we ended up talking about the new barons. Emeric was uncomfortable or unhappy, but that didn't tell me much.

"I can't get into all the reasons now," he said. "You don't have to believe me, just—just try to play this so they keep you here as long as possible. Delay whatever they're planning to do with you. If they bring you someplace else, I don't know if I'll be able to follow."

I glowered at him. "I don't know. That sounds kind of like a plus from where I'm sitting."

He let out a huff of breath. "I need a chance to figure out how we can escape without getting caught while we're getting away. We're nowhere near any of your friends—it's not going to be easy. But no one else here has any interest in your well-being."

"You didn't use to, apparently. Why are you so concerned now?"

His jaw twitched again. "I—I didn't realize—I *tried* to warn you, but you wouldn't even talk to me."

My anger flared back to the surface. I hadn't wanted to talk to him because the last time I'd seen him, he'd tossed me away like a piece of trash. But before any more of that acid could spill onto my tongue, Emeric stood abruptly. Just as his face fell back into its previous emotionless state, the lights blinked on beyond the doorway.

Swinging the tray casually, my supposed co-conspirator sauntered out as if nothing at all unusual had happened. The door thumped shut in his wake. A key rasped in the lock.

I glanced across at Noah. Emeric hadn't said anything about getting the scion free. If he'd been telling the truth, surely he knew there was no way I was leaving unless Noah did too.

Of course, me leaving was a huge "if" all on its own. My anger simmered down until it was a lump of discomfort in my stomach.

Noah had picked up his sandwich and taken a tentative bite, probably to appear as normal as possible. I grabbed my water. My hand balked with the momentary urge to cast a spell to check it for unwelcome chemicals, but I couldn't do that anyway.

If the reapers wanted me dead, they probably wouldn't bother with subtle poisons. All they had to do was walk downstairs and aim a single blast of magic at my head or my heart.

I opened the lid and took a gulp. The cool liquid flowed down my throat, briefly refreshing until it hit the ball of queasiness in my stomach.

"What do you think about this?" I asked Noah, carefully vague.

He considered me, probably thinking back through

the conversation he'd overheard. "Hard to say," he said finally. "I don't think it could hurt to work with what they gave us. We'll just have to wait and see how it goes."

He took another bite as if he'd meant the food, but I assumed he meant Emeric's request too. Play along with the reapers in a way that would keep us here. How the hell were we supposed to do that?

And what if following Emeric's instructions screwed us over even more?

CHAPTER FOUR

Noah

I'd never met either of the men who were interrogating me before this moment, but just a few questions in, I felt reasonably confident in saying they were both jerks. They kept looming over my chair as if they thought I'd be intimidated by their glowers, and the bulky one on the right kept scowling when I took more than a millisecond to compose my answer, as if I was wasting their time. I had to bite my tongue against reminding them that if it'd been up to me, I wouldn't be here at all.

"How are the barons keeping the university secure?" the skinny one asked, tapping his foot against the hardwood floor. Whatever purpose this small room usually served, it was close to the kitchen. The wafting scent of bacon and eggs from our captors' breakfast would have made my mouth water if everything else about my situation hadn't stolen all of my appetite.

A prick of energy against my forehead told me one or the other was probing my mind with a subtle insight spell. I thought deep thoughts about circus elephants and replied in an even voice. "I don't know. The school staff handle that area."

The bulky guy scoffed. "You expect us to believe that the barons haven't asked to be apprised of the wards and other security measures while they're using the school as a safe haven?"

I shrugged as casually as I could with my wrists bound. "I'm not a baron yet, am I? So I wouldn't have been a part of those conversations even if they'd happened."

That wasn't actually true. From the start, my brother and the other full barons had been including the scions old enough to attend Blood U—Agnes Nightwood and me—in most of the business they conducted. It was part of their new egalitarian approach to ruling, and probably a good thing, since I was *way* behind on all the logistics that came with actually being a baron. Up until a couple of years ago, it'd always been clear Declan was going to take on that role alone.

So, yeah, I'd been there when Ms. Grimsworth, the headmistress, had gone over the various layers of magical protection that kept the fearmancer university inaccessible to anyone not explicitly invited to visit. I didn't have any intention of spilling the details to these assholes, though.

The pricking sensation strengthened into a jab. I put all my concentration into pushing forward innocuous images and ideas—a burst of balloons, the Eiffel Tower, the sun beaming over our backyard deck at the main

Ashgrave residence. After the battle with the former barons, Declan had gotten even more paranoid about our *mental* security, and he'd insisted on having me train in non-magical practice techniques for deflecting insight spells, just in case I found myself drained of energy for proper shielding.

I'd thought he was being his usual over-prepared self at the time. Now I was grateful he was such a stickler for caution.

The skinny guy raised an eyebrow. "To what extent do your brother and the other new barons include you in their plans?"

"Not much," I said in the same flippant tone. "They want me to focus on my schooling until I'm of age, which makes sense to me."

The bulky guy leaned in, his eyes glinting. "So, they do tell you a little, then. What subjects have come up recently?"

I couldn't help arching my eyebrows right back at them. "Well, the whole 'conspiracy in Portland' concern was obviously on their minds. You dolts really had no idea what the reapers down there were getting up to until they showed up here, huh?"

I was hoping I might get *them* to spill a few beans— anything at all about what the most prominent reapers had been plotting lately, how organized they were, what they planned to do with Cressida and me now that they had us. But the attempt, like my others during the first interrogation with a different pair of lackeys yesterday, didn't get me very far.

The skinny guy snorted dismissively and ignored my taunt altogether. "You and your brother are quite close. Has he mentioned any tensions between him and the other barons?"

Was he basing that premise on how determinedly Declan had kept me out of the line of fire all these years, or had I accidentally let a stray authentic thought slip through my defenses? I resisted the urge to grit my teeth.

Maybe Declan should have worked me even harder on these techniques. Maybe I should have worked *myself* harder. I could tease him all I liked about his dedication to honing his skills, but that dedication was exactly why he'd been baron material and I'd been the back-up, wasn't it? He'd been preparing for war while I'd been chumming around in Paris. I hardly knew what it was like to really act as a scion, let alone a baron.

I drowned out those self-defeated reflections under another wave of vivid impressions: staring up at the modern art museum, biting into one of those eclairs Cressida loved so much, facing a blast of magic my aunt aimed at me and my brother…

Okay, maybe that last memory wasn't the best one to draw on in this company, but it definitely blared over anything else I might have been thinking of. I let my response tumble off my tongue. "Of course not. The barons are completely united. And they're doing what's best for *all* fearmancers, which maybe you'd recognize if you weren't so concerned only about what's good for you and your friends."

The two men stepped back to mutter to each other. I watched them, my nerves twitching.

How long would they hold onto me here if they weren't making any progress? What if they switched to persuasion spells next? I was pretty adept at talking my way through those—Declan had insisted on even *more* practice there, since he'd seen it as a more likely threat—but it still wouldn't be fun.

I didn't want them giving up completely and moving on to the next stage of their plans just yet, though. They were probably already thinking about moving us. We'd already been here at least a day. The longer we stayed in any one place, the more chance there was that the barons' forces would locate us. But our best chance of getting out of here so far was Emeric, and he'd said we should try to stay here if he was going to pull that off.

He might have been lying through his teeth. It wasn't as if I'd been able to see into his mind without my magic. But specializing in insight included developing a whole lot of nonmagical awareness to supplement the impressions that were often fragmented and confusing. From his posture to the tone of his voice, my regular senses were inclined to believe he was telling the truth.

Which didn't absolve him of the fact that he'd been instrumental in getting us into this predicament in the first place, but we could hash that out as soon as Cressida and I were no longer in chains.

How could I convince these jerks to hang onto us a little longer before dangling me as a hostage before the barons? Could I tempt them with a hint of progress?

When my interrogators turned back to me, I let out a sigh. The skinny one sneered at me. "This should be simple enough. How often does your brother travel between the university and your main residence, and which route does he take?"

"I don't know," I said in a bored tone. "I don't normally make the trip with him, and he goes a lot of places other than those two. You know, being a baron and all." I summoned up a few other vibrant memories from Paris… but I also let my thoughts linger for a moment on a sense of fatigue. *I can hold them off now, but if I'm stuck in that stupid room for even more hours on end, it's going to get harder to stay sharp. What if I can't deflect them well enough next time?*

Energy prickled through my mind. Whichever guy was casting the spell wouldn't have been able to pick up exact words, only the gist of my supposed worry, but that might be enough to make them think it was worth waiting and trying me again after more time had passed.

"You may want to consider being more cooperative," the bulky guy growled. "We might not rough *you* up too much so we're not bartering with damaged goods when it comes to that, but I'm not so sure the girl matters enough to anyone for that to be a concern. Maybe she could use a few bruises to decorate that pretty face."

I managed to suppress the flare of panic that shot up from my gut, using a desperate vision of the first girl I'd ever kissed back in Paris, but it was a near thing. A sour flavor crept into my mouth. "Like you said, she doesn't matter that much. If you think I'd compromise the barony over her, you're even bigger idiots than I already thought."

It was hard to read much in their grim faces, but I thought I'd convinced them. For now. It wasn't entirely untrue that my ability to redirect them would weaken the longer we were stuck in this place.

The bulky guy grabbed my elbow and hauled me to my feet. "I think we'll give you some time to consider your circumstances and how much worse this could get."

It could get a lot worse—I knew that. I suspected if I'd been a full baron and they'd been sure I knew a lot more than I was saying, physical torture might have been on the table after all. It still might be, depending on how they decided I could be most useful to their plans.

But the reaper families had to maintain some kind of front of being the wronged party in the eyes of the larger fearmancer community, especially if they wanted to get the majority of the blacksuits, who acted as both police force and judicial system, back on their side. Carving up a scion would be a little much for even the new barons' harshest critics to stomach.

As my interrogators handed me off to a man who ushered me back down the stairs to the basement, a different sort of discomfort tugged at me. I glanced toward the outer wall automatically.

My familiar was out there—too far away. Kato would have been left behind in Portland. I'd guess Cressida's falcon would follow her here easily enough, wherever here was, but a raccoon couldn't simply soar through clear skies to reach me. I had a sense of him trundling ever nearer, the familiar bond pulling him as much as it did me, but the distance still between us formed a pang in my chest.

That pang only deepened as the man shoved me into the prison room. Cressida looked up where she'd tucked herself into the only corner her chain would allow her to reach. Several strands of her pale hair had straggled free from her usual French braid, and dark circles were forming under her weary eyes. I doubted either of us had gotten the most restful sleep on the cold tiled floor last night.

She held her head up firmly enough, but I could pick up a trace of defeat in the set of her shoulders.

She blamed herself for getting us into this situation. But I was the insight specialist between the two of us. I should have picked up on something being off about Emeric or the other reapers. I'd had days of hanging around in my hotel room with nothing to do *but* go over every facet of our plan and the supposed conspiracy. It'd been my job to keep her safe while she'd been out there in the thick of it.

And I hadn't managed that. I'd even made her feel worse at least once. When I remembered that moment when my ill-advised attempts at flirting had triggered her trauma from her past abuse at the hands of that horrible tutor…

Shame and fury washed through me in a vicious mixture just thinking about it. Cressida had said she didn't want to pursue justice against *that* asshole, that it wasn't worth it after all this time, and I could understand not wanting to dredge up so much awfulness from her past. But any prick who went around taking advantage of his twelve-year-old pupils deserved to be strung up by his tonsils.

At my end of the room, the man pushed me down beside the longer chain and reattached it to my cuffs. He strode out without a word. I let out my breath, wondering if I should make a show of being tired or if that would be laying it on too thick. It might worry Cressida too. I wouldn't be able to tell her it was just a ploy.

No, I'd rather see if I could raise her spirits at least a little.

I aimed a wry smile at her. "How are you hanging in there, *mon petit chou-fleur*?"

The teasing nickname made her lips twitch even though her expression stayed solemn. "You never did tell me how to say broccoli," she reminded me with a cock of her head. "I don't think it's fair that you get to call me silly nicknames and I can't do the same to you."

"Hmm. Come up with something better than copying mine, and maybe I'll give you a quick French lesson."

Just for a moment, a sly light gleamed in her eyes at the challenge. I'd have mentally high-fived myself for the victory if the gleam hadn't faded almost as quickly as it'd appeared. She sagged against the wall again with a slow exhalation. "Tell me some stories about going to school in Paris? Things you *can* tell me?"

Things that couldn't be used against us or the barons by our captors, she meant. I had plenty of tales that would work for that. A patch of warmth bloomed in my chest that she'd asked, that I could do *something* for her in the middle of this disaster. It was a tiny thing, but I'd still give it my all.

"Well," I said, keeping my tone as light as I could, "there was the one time my roommate insisted that we absolutely had to sneak into the Louvre in the middle of the night…"

CHAPTER FIVE

Cressida

I only made it through half of the meal I guessed counted as dinner before I had to push the plate away. The creamy pasta tasted like dust in my mouth. Leaning back against the wall, I closed my eyes and reached out my awareness to my familiar again.

Percy was perched on a tree on the edge of the forest near the chalet. I had a vague sense of his pose and his proximity to me, but it wasn't as if I could see through his eyes and figure out anything about our location that way.

Go back to the university, I thought at him with as much effort as I could put into the idea, picturing the ominous stone buildings of Blood U. *Find Rory—find the barons.* He wasn't going to be able to pass on a message, but if they saw the falcon there, I was pretty sure they'd recognize him as mine. Maybe he'd be able to lead them back to us.

But Percy either didn't understand the orders I was attempting to give him or was unwilling to follow them. The impression I got in return was only a waft of exhaustion after his long flight to reach me and a thread of distress and hopelessness, no doubt because he hadn't been able to actually see me. He could tell I was unhappy, and there was nothing he could do about it.

There is *something you can do*. But communication between mages and familiars was hardly a straightforward process. All he'd be getting from me were similar vague impressions and emotions. Maybe he figured I was just missing Blood U, not that I thought he should go there. It went against a familiar's instincts to leave his bonded mage so far behind, after all.

At least he was here. When he'd gotten some rest, I should be able to encourage him to at least take to the skies. If the barons sent people looking for us and they got close enough, there was a small chance seeing him would point them in the right direction or that he'd realize he should catch their attention.

Too bad the chances of any search party ending up in the right vicinity seemed awfully small too.

I sucked my lower lip under my teeth and held back the urge to worry at it. If I gave in to those anxious impulses, I'd break through the skin before we finished another day.

Noah pushed his own plate aside with a rasp of ceramic over the tiles. When I looked at him, he gave me a sympathetic grimace.

I definitely couldn't tell him what I was trying when

our captors might be listening. No point in getting his hopes up when it'd been a flop so far anyway. I rolled my shoulders, stretching out a little of the deepening stiffness in my muscles, and groped for something I could reasonably say. The silence was starting to gnaw at me.

"How long do you think we'll be stuck here?" I said finally. The reapers had taken him off to talk to him a few times now. I didn't know if he'd seen or heard anything useful—or what he thought of Emeric's suggestion that we should aim to stay here as long as possible now that more time had passed.

Noah paused to consider his answer. "As long as they feel they need to, I guess. Hard to say whether whatever comes next would be better or worse, huh?"

Meaning he thought it could be worse, that we might be better off here. I let myself nibble at my lip just a little. "I don't think we can assume *any* of them care about what happens to us other than how it helps their plans."

Noah shrugged with a slight lift of one corner of his mouth. "I think we can hope that they're not all total monsters, but I wouldn't trust anyone unless that's proven to be true."

He figured it was *possible* Emeric was on our side, then. I wasn't sure how I felt about that. My own hopes lifted at the same time as my stomach clenched.

Noah was way better at reading people than I was—I'd happily admit that. And my observations of Emeric's apology and offer of help had been clouded by anger. But... maybe I didn't *want* Emeric to be sorry. In some weird way, that'd almost make things worse—that he was capable of seeing how horrible he'd been to us, but just hadn't until we were already stuck here at the reapers' mercy.

It'd be easier to deal with him if I could shut him away behind the door labeled "Villains" in my mind, so I could assume everything he did and said came with ill intent.

We hadn't seen him since he'd brought our meals yesterday afternoon. A woman I hadn't recognized had brought down the other food we'd been given. Was that a good sign or a bad one? What if the other reapers had caught on to his trick with the electrical system and kicked him out, and we were already totally out of luck?

Noah shifted his position against the wall and made a face at the door. "They definitely couldn't set a lower standard for entertainment. Maybe they're trying to torture us with boredom."

His blasé tone made my mouth twitch with an almost-smile of my own. Only Noah could make light of the awful situation we'd found ourselves in. As much as I hated that I'd gotten him dragged into this mess, I couldn't help a twinge of gratitude that I wasn't here alone.

If we got out of this okay, I was going to find out the name of that bakery he loved and buy him a whole spread of every French pastry he could imagine.

Imagining that comforted me for about five seconds before my spirits sank again. How likely was it that even one of us would make it out of the reapers' hands unscathed, let alone both of us?

I didn't have much time to contemplate that dark thought. The door squeaked open, and the man with the shaved head who'd ushered me around the chalet before appeared.

With his typical dour expression, he walked over and unlatched me from the wall. An image flickered through my mind of raising my arms and bashing the chain that connected my cuffs against his forehead as hard as I could —but even if I somehow managed to knock him out that way, I didn't have the magic to even get Noah free, let alone make it out of a building that had several other powerful mages on guard.

I curled my fingers into my palms and followed the man out of the room.

The front room with the big picture window where I'd been put on display for the higher reaper families yesterday was empty. Faint strains of classical music carried from somewhere deeper inside the chalet. As my escort led me down a hallway, they dwindled away completely.

He motioned me into a small office-style room with a wooden table and a chair on either side. My nose itched with a whiff of the dust in the air. Apparently they didn't use this space all that frequently. Lucky me.

A bottle of cherry cola was sitting on the table by the far chair. Saliva crept across my tongue at the sight of it. Someone had done their homework—or maybe my dad had noticed my habits under his roof more than he'd shown. That stuff had been one of my favorite treats when I'd wanted a caffeine boost rather than the mellowing of alcohol.

I wasn't going to just accept a random gift from these

assholes, though. I sank into the chair and acted as if I hadn't noticed it, taking in the rest of the room.

The man stepped out, shutting the door behind him, and my back stiffened. The back of the door and the wall around it had pictures taped all over them. Pictures of *me*. Me at the first soiree I'd attended with the Portland reaper families, smiling ingratiatingly at Flora Acheling. Me in that ridiculous harlequin costume, Harriet Mismeren's clown make-up plastered on my face.

Me on my knees, kissing the boot of the guy I'd thought I needed to impress to find out what the reapers' plans for the barons were.

I glanced away from the blown-up printouts, but the memories they'd provoked danced through my mind. Heat prickled over my cheeks. The Portland reapers had gotten to show off all that humiliation—and probably plenty more on video—to Dad and his friends. No wonder the higher reapers figured I was hopeless, useless.

The door swung open again, and the woman from the couple I was pretty sure owned the chalet stalked in. Her tawny hair was swept back in a loose bun and her knob of a chin was raised at the same haughty angle she'd held it while she'd inspected me yesterday. She nudged the door shut behind her and glanced over her shoulder before shooting me a dryly amused glance. "Did you enjoy reminiscing about your past exploits?"

I said nothing. With people like this, the less you gave them the better. But a chill started to spread from my gut up through my chest.

Had they decided what they could use me for after all? If so, just how horrible was that use going to be?

The woman rested her manicured hands on the back of the chair across from me for a moment before tugging it out and sinking into it. She set her elbows on the table and interlaced her fingers beneath her chin. "So. Cressida Warbury. Willing to jump whenever those Portland idiots said "jump" but not for your own family."

I glowered at her, still silent. She knew why I'd gone along with the Portland reapers' demands—and it was the exact same reason I *hadn't* lived up to my parents' expectations.

Unless they didn't know for sure? Was she trying to gauge how committed I was to the new barons?

Either way, the best answer was still none at all.

Unfortunately, I didn't have a whole lot of choice in the matter. The woman's lips moved with the softest casting word, a tingle passed over my scalp, and her mouth curved into a smirk. "Annoying you, am I? Speak up, and this can be over faster."

She'd cast an insight spell on me. I had no magical barrier against it right now. Crap, what if Emeric really was trying to help us and she pulled *that* out of my mind?

As soon as the possibility occurred to me, I trained my attention away from all memory of Emeric. Suddenly I was very fascinated by the grain of wood on the table, the faint wrinkles that lined the tan skin around the woman's elbows.

"What exactly do you want me to speak about?" I

asked. If I gave a show of playing along, that might mean she delved less into my head.

"Oh, I'm just wondering what sort of reward those treacherous barons offered that would be enough to sway a previously devout fearmancer like yourself to their side. Look at them, so willing to put you through so much humiliation on their behalf." She tsked. "You must be getting quite a lot out of that for yourself."

Yeah, I got friends—or at least allies—who weren't constantly evaluating whether they'd get more value out of stabbing me in the back than playing nice. The fact that these jerks called themselves "loyalists" was ridiculous. The only people the reapers were loyal to were themselves.

"Maybe I just enjoy their company," I said flatly.

She made a scoffing sound. "An awfully low price. But I can see why they'd entrust you with tasks like this 'mission' if you're so easily bought."

What exactly was she trying to get at? So far this conversation had seemed to mostly be for the purpose of taking jabs at me.

I spread my hands, keeping my tone even. "I don't know. What's it matter to you? Don't you have better things to do than poke fun at some worthless traitor who got so easily duped?"

"You were angry about that." A statement, not a question. "No matter who you throw your lot in with, you're going to get used."

"If that's supposed to be a pitch for switching back over to your side, I'll pass."

Her lip curled into more of a sneer, but it was actually

kind of a relief not to have to pretend I gave a shit what these people thought of me like I had in Portland. With a sudden rush of defiance, I opened the cherry cola bottle and took a swig of the sharply sweet soda. It fizzed down my throat into my stomach. I couldn't say I was savoring it, but if it'd been an attempt at winning me over, I'd happily enjoy it while treating her subtle offer like the crap it was.

The woman's expression turned even haughtier. "I suppose the barons should be glad they've found such a devoted sycophant, then, for however long they hold onto their thrones." She stood up. "Not that you're likely to ever see them again with that kind of attitude."

I gulped more of the cola, but the fizz felt more nauseating than uplifting now. They were simply going to kill me, were they? Or keep me around to see how much more they could humiliate me until they got bored—and *then* kill me?

"Sorry that you haven't been more inspiring," I retorted, hiding the icy tension spreading through my limbs.

The woman chuckled and walked out of the room without another word.

Now what? I sat for several minutes, sipping the cherry cola and letting my gaze wander over the parts of the room that weren't plastered with the embarrassing highlights of my recent life. There was a cupboard near me that proved locked when I tugged on its door. The shelving unit behind me only held a few paperbacks with creased covers. No one else came in to check on or harass me.

Was this some other step in their plan? An attempt at wearing me down?

I must have been in there longer than I'd realized, because my head was starting to feel muggy with fatigue despite the caffeine in the cola. I drained the last of it to no effect. My head drooped, and my eyelids with it.

Well, if I took a little nap here, at least I'd be getting some rest for myself instead of playing more of the reapers' games.

Arranging my arms in as comfortable a position as I could with my wrists cuffed, I laid my head on them and closed my eyes. I was briefly aware of the dimples in the tabletop and the sour-sweet aftertaste in my mouth turning increasingly bitter, and then I was out like a light.

CHAPTER SIX

Cressida

My shoulder swayed, and the rest of my body swayed with it. A hand gripped me, shaking me.

My pulse stuttered, but my eyes opened sluggishly, as if a magnetic force was dragging the lids back down. My thoughts felt sluggish too, as if my head were full of tar. A prickling sensation ran over my gums. My mouth was parched.

When I managed to focus, I found Emeric crouched beside me, his face shadowed in the darkness. No light was falling from the overhead window, only a thin wash seeping past the door that stood partly ajar. He turned his head, and a gleam of the dim illumination caught in the widened whites of his eyes.

"Come on," he whispered urgently. "We have to go *now*."

With a jolt of adrenaline, I realized the weight on my wrists was gone. A glimmer of magic tickled the space between my lungs. I dragged in a relieved gulp of air and hefted myself upright, reaching to rub the chaffed skin below my hands.

Noah was already up—on his feet, unchained and uncuffed, his stance wary but determined. We were really doing this—we were getting out of here?

Before my mind had totally caught up in its muddled state, Emeric tugged me the rest of the way onto my own feet. His voice rasped, barely audible even in the stillness of the night. "Just follow me. I arranged a distraction, but it won't last forever."

In that first instant, my legs balked instinctively. The man grasping my arm had manipulated me, humiliated me, treated me like trash, and offered me up to my worst enemies. Why the hell would I go anywhere with *him*?

But I couldn't really imagine any situation *worse* than the one I was already in. What did I have to lose? Letting him break us out of this prison didn't mean I trusted him.

I propelled myself forward, Noah hurrying along beside me. The scion shot me a flash of a smile, small but encouraging, that settled my nerves just a little. If he didn't think going with Emeric was a ridiculous idea, then we were probably okay.

I set my bare feet as quietly as I could on the cool basement floor. Emeric's and Noah's shoes made a faint clomping that set me on edge all over again. My gaze darted along the hall. I half expected the chalet staff to come hurtling toward us, hands blazing with spells.

But we made it to the stairs unaccosted. Emeric slowed there, cocking his head as he pulled farther in front of us. He had a large backpack slung over his shoulders—what was he carrying in there?

As we reached the first floor, distant voices reached my ears. They sounded as if they were coming from the back of the building. There was a crackling noise and a startled exclamation. That was Emeric's distraction, I guessed.

Emeric peered around and motioned for us to hustle to the front door. He muttered a few casting words under his breath and then pushed it open. Fresh foresty air flooded over me—I inhaled deeply, letting it steady my mind.

The grit on the front steps and on the asphalt beyond bit into the soles of my feet, but I wasn't going to complain about that right now. Emeric headed straight to a modest compact car parked near the far end of the circular drive. Not his, apparently, because he opened it not with a key fob but another hastily murmured word.

He tossed his bag into the passenger seat and motioned us into the back. "Get in and get down!"

Noah leapt in first, and I clambered after him. I shut the door as gently as I could, my heart thudding, and then sank down so my head rested on the middle seat. A faintly oily, salty scent like stale potato chips crept into my nose.

Noah ducked down too. He braced himself carefully against his elbow so that he didn't lean right on me, but when he rested a tentative hand on my arm, I reached to squeeze his hand. Right now I didn't care about anything other than the fact that we were getting out of here—both of us.

Emeric's shoulders stiffened as he spoke the words to spark the ignition. The engine rumbled to life, its vibration carrying through the fabric of the seat. As he eased out of the parking spot and turned the car toward the road, I held my breath. My ears strained for any hint of a problem beyond the vehicle's walls.

So far so good. Emeric shifted from reverse into drive and slowly pressed down on the gas. The car cruised forward—

—and a shout that sounded way too close broke through the thrum of the engine.

"Shit!" Emeric cursed under his breath. "Hold on."

He slammed on the gas, and Noah and I both jerked back in our seats. The suspension rocked with a sharp turn. The car careened onward with the engine roaring now, and I clutched Noah's sleeve as if holding on for dear life.

"We still have a good chance," Emeric said, his words blurring together as they spilled from his mouth. "I deflated a tire on each of the other cars—they won't be able to—"

Something smacked into the rear of the car with an electric sizzle, and the suspension hitched. The engine sputtered. Emeric swore again, pumping the gas pedal, but the thrum kept dwindling. He spat out one casting word after another, but none of them stopped the car from grinding to a halt.

My heart outright stopped. "They hit us with a spell?"

"Yeah. Shit. I…" Emeric muttered a couple more casting words to no effect and then slammed his hands on the steering wheel. It sounded as if the titanium one hit it hard enough to leave a dent. "Okay. Plan B—out of the car and into the forest. Move as fast as you can. The farther we can get from the road, the better."

Neither Noah nor I was in much position to argue. When I shoved the back door open, the banging of other doors carried from back by the chalet. The reapers must be figuring out that they couldn't drive after us right now, but it'd only be a matter of time before they followed on foot. I could still see the gleam of the chalet's lights up the road. We'd barely made it a quarter of a mile.

Emeric hauled his pack over his shoulders again and leapt the ditch to plunge into the brush on the other side. Noah and I followed, Noah holding my elbow. As twigs and sharp pebbles nicked my feet, I bit back a gasp, but I couldn't hide my wince. Noah shot me a worried glance, but I shook my head and dashed onward, clenching my teeth against the pain. I'd be in a hell of a lot more if the reapers got their hands on me.

Emeric led us on a diagonal route, taking us both away from the road and farther from the chalet. The darkness thickened between the trees, only flickers of moonlight penetrating the thick foliage overhead. He was little more than a vague shape ahead of us, swerving this way and that to avoid a tree or a particularly thick clump of brushes, heaving himself over a mossy log.

Animals I couldn't see scattered in our wake, tiny glimmers of fear shooting into my chest at the terror our passing provoked. I gathered that energy at the base of my throat and murmured a casting word of my own, calling the illusion of thicker shadows around us. Even the beam of a flashlight—magical or otherwise—shouldn't be able to reveal us through that conjured cloak.

"Is there anything you can do to dampen the noise we're making?" I asked both my companions in a hushed voice. An illusion couldn't create silence where there was none, and I didn't trust my lesser physicality skills and weakened stores of magic to be up to the job.

I barely made out Emeric's jerk of a nod. "Yes. Right." As we hurried onward, he intoned several syllables under his breath. The crackling of the brush and the thumping of our feet dulled even to my ears. He let out a soft, shaky laugh. "They'll have to be practically on top of us to hear us now. For at least a little while."

How much magic did he have stored up? I doubted he'd been scaring much of anyone among the fearmancers back in the chalet. My father and his friends had appeared to find the Portland families more of an irritation than anything else.

Each step sent fresh jabs through my feet—but Emeric's spell hadn't dampened any sounds other than our own, and there was a distant crunching from behind as pursuers barged into the woods after us. My pulse stuttered, and I pushed myself even faster.

What *would* they do to us if they caught us? Noah they'd probably just haul back to the prison room and tighten his chains, but it hadn't seemed like I was worth much to them. At this point, I wouldn't be surprised if they figured it was easiest to kill me. And they hadn't cared about Emeric to begin with, as far as I could tell. If this wasn't some incredibly convoluted set-up, if he really was doing his best to help us escape, then he'd betrayed the reapers even worse than I ever had.

He might have signed his death warrant the second he unlocked us from our restraints.

I swallowed hard and kept tramping after him as fast as my throbbing feet would go. My chest was starting to tighten, my breaths coming shorter. I hadn't exactly gotten a lot of cardio in over the past few weeks, let alone the past two days of doing not much more than sitting, and the uneven terrain with its natural obstacles made for exhausting trekking.

At least I could take a little comfort in the fact that it wouldn't be much more enjoyable for the reapers chasing after us.

Emeric gave a sharp wave of his hand and swung farther to his right. Noah squeezed my elbow, and we hustled after him. Several paces later, he slowed to pick his way down a steep slope scattered with fallen leaves.

"Brush the leaves back into place behind us," he whispered. "We don't want it to be obvious we came this way."

Noah turned to follow his instructions. I just focused on staying upright and tuning out how much my feet were hurting.

When we hit flatter ground at the base of the slope, Emeric headed onward in the same direction for a few minutes. Then he motioned us over to a dense cluster of tall shrubs to his left. We pushed between them and found a small clearing. It made a tight fit for the three of us, but it gave us a little more shelter from searching eyes.

I murmured my shadow-thickening spell again to bolster its effect, and Emeric dug into his backpack. He thrust a couple of shapes toward me that I only recognized as sneakers in the near-blackness when my hands closed around their canvas and rubber surface.

"Sorry," he said roughly. "I was going to give them to you in the car once we'd gotten some distance, but there wasn't any time."

Yeah, I'd take my battered feet over having my whole self battered if the reapers had caught up with us. Wobbling and grimacing at the pain, I wriggled one shoe on and then the other. They felt a couple of sizes too big— where had Emeric gotten them? Stolen from one of the chalet's staff?—and they definitely didn't match my dress, as if I gave a fuck about that. All that mattered to me at this point was getting some kind of barrier between my skin and the forest floor.

My soles still throbbed against the thinly cushioned interior of the sneakers, but at least they wouldn't take any further damage. A bit of dampness on my fingers afterward made me wonder if they were outright bleeding, but I couldn't bring myself to worry about that either.

A tug of eager concern reverberated through me. Percy. My head jerked up automatically, although I couldn't make out more than snatches of sky through the leaves above us. I could sense him, though, swooping through the air, tracking his impression of me below him...

A fresh splash of panic hit me. If the reapers could see him against the night sky, he'd help lead them to our current position.

Come to me, I thought at my familiar, keeping the vibe of my encouraging call as warm and welcoming as possible despite the skittering of my nerves. *Come down through the trees.*

Percy might not want to journey all the way back to Blood U alone, but he was perfectly happy to come *closer* to me. I felt him dive toward the forest canopy.

"We should keep moving," Emeric was saying quietly. "We can't give them—"

I held up my hand to stop him, focusing on my awareness of Percy. A few moments later, the falcon landed on a nearby branch with only the softest tap of his talons. I sent a waft of gratitude his way and gestured to Emeric. "My familiar needs some of that silencing magic too."

As Emeric did his thing, I worked a little more of my own magic to drape shadows around Percy. Then I nodded. "All right, let's go."

"Wait." Noah shifted beside me. I could barely make out his face in the darkness, let alone the expression on it, but he was so close his shoulder brushed mine. I felt more than saw his attention on me. "We should check for any kind of tracking spell the reapers might have cast on us. No good running away if they can follow us no matter what we do."

Right, of course. Even a basic spell cast while we slept might draw them to us at this short a distance, and we couldn't count on getting far enough away to be out of range before they descended on us.

I held still while Noah murmured a spell that tingled over my body from head to toe. "Good," he said with some relief. "Nothing on you is giving off any kind of magical energy."

"I'll check you," I said before Emeric could offer. I might have been willing to follow him this far, but that didn't mean I wanted to count on him for every aspect of our security. "We should probably make sure there's nothing on him too."

Emeric didn't protest. I sent a questing tendril of magic over Noah's form first, seeking out any trace of supernatural energy emitting from him, and when he proved clear, he confirmed Emeric was as well. The other guy's stance had become increasingly tense. "I wouldn't risk staying here any longer."

I waved toward the forest. "We're good. Let's go."

We headed off again, my feet chaffing in the overlarge sneakers but with nowhere near as much discomfort as had come from walking barefoot. Emeric set a brisk pace that soon had sweat trickling down my back even though the night air had cooled the August warmth. Percy flapped from tree to tree alongside us, staying well out of sight.

Once, I heard a voice so far off that I couldn't distinguish the words even though it had the tone of a yell. We walked even faster after that, but it was the last hint of our pursuers that reached us.

For now. I kept up the rhythm of one foot after the other, but fatigue was already eating away at the adrenaline that'd propelled me this far. Anxious questions crept in with it.

How far would we have to go to really be safe? And what else might we run into in this vast forest that could be just as dangerous as the mages behind us?

CHAPTER SEVEN

Emeric

I glowered at the plump mushroom sprouting between two tree roots. For what wasn't the first time in the past half an hour, I wished I'd added a few wilderness survival skills to my physicality studies. For example, learning how to detect natural poisons in a plant or, well, mushroom would have come in very handy right now.

We had to eat *something*. When I'd made my escape plan, I hadn't counted on being stuck in the wilderness for who knew how long. I'd stuffed a few apples and a box of crackers I'd nabbed from the Kingsleys' kitchen into my backpack in case we needed more fuel on the road, but we'd made short work of those in our hasty breakfast before we'd gotten a little rest this morning. The day was now past lunchtime and well on its way toward dinner, and my stomach had condensed into a dull ache of hunger.

Cressida and her scion friend were working on the problem too, but I was the one who'd gotten us into this situation—both being trapped at the Kingsleys in the first place and adrift in the woods now. If I'd hustled us out of the house a little faster... if I'd arranged my distraction a little more effectively... We'd been maybe a hundred feet from the bend in the road where the car would have zoomed out of view of whichever mage had thrown that engine-frying spell at it.

I swiped the mushroom and dropped it into my bag just in case. Maybe one of my fellow escapees would have some idea whether it was edible.

As I straightened up, I swiped at the sweat that'd formed on my brow. The mid-summer heat filled the air even beneath the shelter of the treetops—if anything, it might have been worse than out in the open where there'd have been more of a breeze. I felt like I was baking in an oven.

Of course, it could've been worse. We could have been tramping around out here in January.

Or not, because if it'd been January, we'd either have been caught or frozen into icicles by now.

I pushed onward through the brush, ignoring the scratch of twigs through my shirt sleeves, scanning the nearby bushes and tree branches for any kind of score: wild fruit, a bird's nest with eggs. I wasn't going to be picky.

A little while later, I stumbled on a small clearing where the ground was spotted with clover. I'd never chowed down on the plant myself, but if it didn't kill horses, it should be okay for us, right? I gathered a bunch of the stuff to add to my pathetic stash.

While on my clover spree, I accidentally snapped off a stem of another plant that gave off a surprising garlicky smell. For the hell of it, I gathered as many of those as I could too. I had a vague memory of Mom telling us once about picking wild garlic when she was a kid living out in the country.

It wasn't likely to fill us up, but at least we'd get a little flavor with our meager pickings.

By the time I was finished in the clearing, my nerves had started to twitch with the awareness of how long I'd been gone from our makeshift camp. I paused to murmur a quick searching spell to confirm no one other than my expected companions was anywhere nearby.

We'd cast out wards at a good distance around the spot that were meant to alert us if any other human being passed them, but I didn't trust people like the Kingsleys or Cressida's father not to have tricks I couldn't anticipate up their sleeves. That was why they had the fancy chalets and the big bank accounts while families like mine made do with picking up whatever scraps of work we could get on the fringes of fearmancer society, right?

The forest around me looked pretty much the same in every direction, but the tug of another spell led me back to our camp. As I got closer, I caught a whiff of woodsmoke and… Was that roasting meat?

I picked up my pace and hurried into the small glade to find Cressida and the Ashgrave scion crouched by a small fire. It must have been conjured magically, because I couldn't see any of us having the backwoods skills to whittle a flame out of two sticks. One of them had assembled a rough spit that dangled two carcasses that looked vaguely pigeon-like.

"How the hell did you get those?" I blurted out before I could think better of my tone.

Cressida had looked almost relaxed when I'd arrived. The second I spoke, her expression hardened the way it had when I'd brought lunch to her two days ago.

"My familiar caught them for us," she said tartly, turning her attention back to the fire. "It only took a little encouragement. He doesn't like knowing I'm hungry. If he can grab another bird, we'll each get one."

Somehow I suspected if we were stuck with just two, she'd happily share the bounty with just the scion and leave me to my own scavenged offerings. The smell of the meat made my stomach gurgle, and I winced inwardly. And not just because of the embarrassingly obvious indication of my hunger. A thinner but sharper pang ran through my chest, as it had repeatedly over the past few days.

I'd had to leave my own familiar behind in Portland. A bearded dragon, even one made hardier by the magic that'd formed our connection, wasn't the type of animal you could easily cart around on multi-hour drives. I'd figured he was safer at home. One of my father's friends had always been willing to check in on and feed him when I'd made my trips out to Blood U to drop Shauna off.

As I hunkered down on the ground on the other side of the fire, the falcon swooped down through the trees and dropped another limp, feathered body next to Cressida, saving me from any blatant gestures of exclusion. Noah immediately picked up the bird, which looked like a dove, and started plucking the feathers out with just a hint of a grimace.

The scion had at least a little grit to him, I'd admit to myself. Or maybe hunting was one of the many posh barony family pastimes I wouldn't know anything about.

"I found a couple of blackberry bushes," he said as he worked, his gaze fixed on the bird. "They weren't too picked over by the wildlife, so I brought back a decent amount."

For all my searching, they'd both come up with more than I had. I willed back the prickle of irritation at that fact and opened up my pack. "I guess I'm supplying the greens, then. If we're desperate enough. I figured we could do a clover salad, and I found some wild garlic. Also a few mushrooms that I'm not sure are edible."

"Let's not risk it," Cressida said briskly. "But I won't turn down clover and garlic salad if it gives us a little more energy." She poked at the fire again, her gaze traveling up over the path of the smoke, and intoned a casting word under her breath that summoned enough of a breeze to disperse it before it reached the leaves overhead.

She was savvy enough to take precautions like that even though I doubted her family had been much of one for camping trips. I didn't mind giving her due credit anywhere near as much as I did with the Ashgrave guy.

I left my backpack where it was and grabbed the three now-empty water bottles I'd brought for our trip. It'd seemed like plenty when I'd dropped them into my bag— the joke was on me. "I'll fill these up while the birds are cooking."

We'd chosen this spot to stop partly because we were all pretty wiped out by the time the sun had peeked through the trees, partly because it'd seemed safer to rest during the day and be on the move at night when we wouldn't be as visible, and partly because we'd happened to stumble on a sizeable stream burbling through the woods. It was only a couple of feet deep and a few across, but the water was moving quickly enough and looked clear enough that I figured drinking it was better than dying of dehydration.

I dunked each of the bottles into the water until they were full, enjoying the cool current against my regular hand. Then I swiped a little over my face and around the back of my neck to take the edge off the heat. My T-shirt was clinging to my chest more than I'd like. If I didn't stink already, I probably would soon enough. It hadn't occurred to me to bring a change of clothes either.

We were supposed to already be back at Blood U by now—or wherever Cressida would have asked me to drop her and the scion off if we'd kept going in the car.

Fuck, everything had gone so wrong. I'd hassled her enough over what I'd imagined was her desire to play hero with the new barons, but I'd screwed up my own attempt at heroics pretty epically.

When I returned to the camp, Cressida had taken the first two birds off the fire, and Noah was just stringing the third into place over the flames. As I'd have expected, they each took one of the cooked birds, but the scion set the blackberries he'd gathered on an indented stone in the middle of our loose cluster where I could reach them too. I allowed myself to take a tentative handful.

Cressida pried off a charred wing and nibbled at the flesh. The relief on her face suggested it didn't taste half as bad as she'd been prepared for. After a few more bites and a gulp of stream water, she shifted her gaze toward the descending sun. "So, is the plan that we just keep walking? How far is it to the nearest town around here?" Her attention came back to me, warily. "I'm not even sure what state we're in."

Of course she wasn't. Out of the fear that we'd draw the reapers hunting for us our way, we hadn't talked during the night except for our hushed spells, and we'd been too exhausted when we'd stopped to do more than cast our wards and collapse in the basic shelters we'd constructed out of fallen branches, leaves, and a little magic to hold it all together.

I swallowed the last of the sharply sweet berries. "Upstate Maine. There's not much of anything for miles, unfortunately. When we were driving, I think we went at least an hour without seeing anything but forest before we made it to the Kingsleys' house."

"The Kingsleys," Cressida repeated to herself, and I realized that she hadn't known who her "hosts" were either.

Noah grimaced more overtly this time. "We can't be making much better time than two or three miles an hour walking through this kind of terrain. Maybe less at night when we can't see as well. I don't suppose you brought a map."

"I thought I'd be able to count on my phone." I pulled the device from my pocket and held it up, but like every other time I'd checked, it showed no reception bars at all. Not surprising, considering I'd barely gotten one at the chalet itself. "And I thought I wouldn't need a map until we were through this stretch and into semi-civilization. The road was pretty clear."

Cressida sucked her lower lip under her teeth in a way that reminded me far too well of what it was like to kiss that soft mouth. A jolt of heat shot to my groin, as if lust had any place in our current situation.

It might not have any place in my life at all from now on when it came to her. I couldn't help letting my gaze linger on her as she stared thoughtfully into the flames. Her dress might be wrinkled, her pale hair coming loose from its braid, but she didn't look remotely beaten. The determination etched all over her face made her as stunning as some kind of warrior goddess.

I hadn't appreciated that strength in her before. I hadn't appreciated just how much of a survivor she was. Like me, except in ways I had to admit I didn't fully understand, even after seeing the way her father looked at her and spoke to her.

This woman was tough, practical, and resilient, but she hadn't let any of the beatings she'd taken—emotional or otherwise—turn her sour.

No, there'd been enough sweetness and compassion in the way she'd responded to me across the time we'd spent together in Portland that I'd started feeling twinges of guilt about my plans even before I'd realized how horrible a mistake I'd made. Everything in me longed to revel in her strength, to show her I could match her better than some pretty-boy scion.

But I'd ruined any chance I might have had, hadn't I? Too caught up in the reaper rhetoric and the bitterness that'd been consuming me over the past two years. Not that I was going to apologize for the bitterness—I'd earned it. But she hadn't deserved it aimed at *her*.

As if she'd sensed my thoughts, Cressida's eyes twitched my way. She took another bite, chewed it slowly, and then said, "If we're going to be traveling together for a while, I think we'd better get some things out in the open. Starting with, why the fuck did you drag us into that sick plan of yours in the first place?"

I couldn't deny it was a reasonable question. That didn't mean I was looking forward to answering it. I dropped my own gaze for a moment, sorting through all the explanations and apologies I'd imagined in my head, trying to find the one that felt as if it'd work out the best.

I honestly had no idea, but I had to say something. I forced myself to meet her eyes. "I'm sorry. So incredibly sorry. I—things have been tough since the battle between the barons, and I ended up resenting everyone on the other side, and the only way to make things better for us seemed to be proving myself to the other reaper families in town..." I rubbed my forehead. "It was a shitty thing to do, but that was how I justified it to myself."

"You told yourself I was an awful traitor who deserved whatever I got."

I winced outwardly at that remark, accurate as it was. But my hackles came up at the same time. "All I knew was you'd gone over to the other side and fought with them without seeming like it bothered you to ditch the rest of us, and you jumped at the chance to play hero for the new barons all over again. I was working with the information I had."

"Which was hardly anything, so you shouldn't have assumed anything from it, let alone dragged me into some crazy plot that could get me *killed*." She glared at me. "I didn't even jump at the chance—I almost didn't do it. But I felt like I owed the barons, who've done a hell of a lot more for me than I have for them, and I wanted to be more than just a turncoat. Just because your head is full of nonsense about how horrible the scions were for turning against their families doesn't mean that's true either, you know."

She'd told me in her sort-of confession that the new barons had been more welcoming than the reapers ever had been. Clearly that included her own family. I still found it hard to wrap my head around that version of history. I'd seen them at the final battle—they'd looked nothing short of wrathful. Against their own parents, over what? Not having enough say in fearmancer politics yet?

I hadn't been all that keen on the whispers I'd been hearing about how the old barons were starting to impose on Naries openly, but there had to have been better ways of resolving the disagreement.

I bit back those sentiments, swallowing hard. Probably there was more I didn't know on that subject too. But I couldn't help saying one thing on the subject. "They didn't seem all that great while they were burning off my arm and killing my father."

Cressida hesitated, her jaw clenching. Her voice came out not exactly gentle, but at least less angry. "Your father died in that fight. You never said anything."

I turned to face the fire, running my fingers through my hair. "I didn't want you wondering more than you might have already why I'd turn to the new barons for help after everything that happened. But yes. He died, and I lost half my arm, and my mom had already flown the coop years ago, so it was just me and my sister. I wasn't trying to make my way up in the world just for fun. I had to make sure she'd be okay."

"Your sister's still at Blood U."

I gave a jerk of a nod. "She's only sixteen. She enrolled after the fighting was over. We couldn't afford private tutors—I wasn't going to stop her from learning to use her magic over which barons the administration sided with."

Shauna had *offered* not to go. Had cried in the car on our first trip out there at the thought that she'd be taking classes with people who'd been fighting against me and Dad, maybe even the mage who'd killed him… But the idea of trying to figure it all out herself, of falling so far behind in her skills, had frightened her even more.

I hadn't let her refuse for my sake. Dad wouldn't have wanted her making that sacrifice either.

She'd gotten quieter over the past year and a half when

she'd come home. I'd assumed she simply didn't want to tell me about the bad parts. Was it possible she'd actually started to *like* the atmosphere there and was afraid that if she admitted she'd noticed a lot of good to the place, I'd be mad at her?

The thought made my stomach flip over. I closed my eyes for a second, rubbing them with the heels of my hands. Then I looked at Cressida again. "I know what I did was fucked up, and that I totally misjudged you—and it'd probably have been fucked up even if you *had* been some snotty bitch who didn't care about anything except your own ego. I'm trying to make up for it by getting you back where you belong. Obviously that hasn't gone great so far, but… I *am* trying."

The scion had watched the entire exchange in calm silence. Now he took the last bird off its spit and held it out. As I accepted it cautiously, he studied me. "How did you trick the barons into believing you were genuine? Malcolm did his persuasive interrogation on you. I know my brother would have been checking for signs of deceit using insight too."

I shrugged. That part was easy enough to talk about. "I practiced a ton before I went in there, focusing on specific thoughts and impressions in response to the topics they were likely bring up. Figuring out the questions they'd probably ask and how I could answer them truthfully without revealing anything I didn't want to. It's not *that* hard if you're prepared and you don't have to withstand prolonged questioning. You all coached Cressida to face the reapers in just a couple of days."

Cressida's mouth tightened. She started eating again, gazing at the fire rather than me. I hadn't touched the crisped bird in my hands yet.

"Look," I said, hating that I needed to spell this out but knowing I had to, "I understand you might never want to see me again once we get out of these woods. I realize there'll be a trial with the blacksuits, and I just hope the new barons are as wonderful as you seem to think and take into account that I brought you back to them. But I *will* bring you back, even if you hate me. We've shown we can find food. We've got magic to protect us. As long as we stay ahead of the reapers, we'll make it out of this mess."

"I don't have much choice, do I?" Cressida said, her phrasing and the edge in her voice taking away any pleasure I might have gotten out of her agreement.

CHAPTER EIGHT

Cressida

Noah stopped in a clearer patch of forest to wipe his arm across his forehead and murmur a couple of casting words. His eyes turned briefly hazy as he focused on the impressions he was getting from his spells. Then he clapped his hands together with the wryly optimistic energy he'd been keeping up since we'd set out again after sunset. "Still heading in the right direction."

In the darkness a few feet to my right, Emeric nodded. We'd been stopping every half hour or so to confirm that we hadn't veered off track. It wasn't possible to do any kind of finely targeted casting at the distance we were working with, but human civilization gave off enough energy of various sorts that it wasn't too hard to at least determine where the closest town lay. When I'd done the casting, I'd sensed it like a faint, vague humming up ahead.

That hum hadn't gotten all that stronger in the three nights we'd been traveling like this now, but I was trying not to let that get me down. We clearly still had a lot of ground to cover before we significantly closed the gap.

We set off again, walking as quickly as we dared over the uneven terrain. I'd already stubbed my toes twice. The soles of my feet still ached a bit from that initial dash barefoot two nights ago, not to mention the old and newer blisters from the ill-sized sneakers. I'd cast a numbing spell on my skin before we'd headed out, but it'd faded.

My gaze slid to the right again, but not to look at Emeric. Somewhere a good trek in that direction lay the road into the town we were aiming for. It'd have been a hell of a lot easier—and faster—walking on the asphalt. Emeric might even have been able to get a phone signal. But the reapers had to be patrolling that road more than anywhere else, and we'd be easy to spot if we emerged from the forest. Who knew what magical wards they might have laid out that could trip us up as well?

So we'd decided we were better off going slow and awkward but safe through the woods. I didn't regret that decision, but I did wish it hadn't been the right one.

Noah strode along at my left as if there wasn't anything he'd rather have been doing than hiking through a stretch of isolated forest without so much as a dirt path. Even when he tripped on a stone hidden in the dark and had to grope for a branch to steady himself, he shot a mock grimace at me afterward that quickly transformed into a grin. I couldn't help grinning back at him, as little as I was enjoying this hike.

He'd never seemed like one to stew about things he couldn't change anyway, but I had the feeling he was making a particular effort to stay optimistic for my benefit. He wasn't aiming those grins at Emeric. A twinge of affection ran through my chest. No matter where we were or what hell we'd been through, he was still looking out for me every way he could.

Why had I been so *stupid* and let one drunken urge taint everything I could have had with him? As much warmth as filled me with his presence, the twist of guilt always lurked behind it—the knowledge that I'd been his teacher's aide and his tutor, and fallen into bed with him out of my own selfish desires. Just like—

I gritted my teeth at the memory of Shane Harrowfell gazing down at me when I was wearing that awful harlequin outfit at the costume ball. Of his casual detachment, like the encounter meant nothing to him, like he hadn't defiled me dozens of times over in the two years he'd been *my* tutor ages ago.

Thank god he hadn't come along to the gathering at the chalet. If there *was* any god seeing justice done, my reveal of his crime—under a spell persuading me to tell the truth, no less—would mean he was shunned from any social circle the Achelings were a part of for the rest of time.

We reached a narrow groove in the ground, what looked like it might have been a streambed once now dried up. Noah offered me his hand to help me pick my way across the gap. He squeezed my fingers for just a second before letting go and turned his gaze toward the leaves overhead. They rustled with the humid breeze, revealing glimpses of the starry sky. His voice came out in a whisper. "Such a lovely night for a stroll, *ma chérie*."

I muffled a snort with the back of my hand. Emeric shook his head as he followed us, but he didn't make any comment. We'd all been staying pretty quiet in general, even though we hadn't caught any sign of the reapers nearby since our initial mad dash through the woods.

It wasn't much longer before my stomach started to pinch. The food I'd consumed during the past day had added up to about one full meal. I pulled one of the wild garlic shoots Emeric had collected more of out of my pocket and chewed on it while I walked. It only took a slight edge off my hunger, but that was better than nothing, and there was something satisfying about having some kind of culinary flavor in my mouth.

I obviously shouldn't be kissing anyone anytime soon, but I hadn't been planning on that anyway.

Noah pulled a little ahead, walking faster with a sudden eager urgency I didn't totally understand—until a fat, furry body scampered out of the brush to leap at him. He caught his raccoon familiar in his arms, and Kato promptly clambered up his chest to perch on his shoulder, tugging playfully at the strands of his hair. A soft laugh escaped Noah. When he swiveled to face us, he was outright beaming.

"Quite the intrepid adventurer," he said, ruffling the raccoon's thick fur. "If he made it all the way out here from Portland, I think we should be able to handle the march to some kind of town."

"If only we were as built for forest travel as he is," I muttered, but I was smiling too. It must have been niggling at Noah for ages, being separated from his familiar. I'd bet Kato had barely stopped to rest during his trek, he'd have been so determined to close the gap in their bond.

Noah gave the raccoon one more pat and started walking again, letting Kato keep his shoulder perch. "I think he needs a break from exploring, but when he's up to it, I'll see if he can't find us some edible stuff like Percy has. All familiars must pull their weight."

I thought I caught a flex of Emeric's jaw. Right, his familiar was nowhere nearby. He'd told me he had a bearded dragon—would it have lived in a tank most of the time like the snake familiars a few of my classmates had kept? It might not even be able to try to come to him, whether that would be wise in the first place or not.

Part of me wanted to come up with something reassuring to say, but the other, larger parts were too weary to come up with anything convincing and too unsettled by my history with the guy to bother.

Several feet ahead of us, Percy launched himself from one tree to another. The itch to soar up into the open air above the canopy trickled from him into me, and I sent my apologies his way. Even at night, I didn't want to risk him drawing the reapers to our general location. The stars were bright enough that he'd be visible against the sky.

We'd just keep going, keep not starving, keep

swallowing the discomforts, and eventually we'd come out of this okay. Right?

I'd only just thought that when my foot plunged half a foot farther than I'd expected that patch of ground to go. I pitched forward, stumbling out of the dip that'd been hidden in the darkness, and my ankle rolled. Pain shot from my heel all the way to my calf. Hissing, I hopped on my uninjured foot to grab a sapling for balance.

The guys had come to a stop on either side of me. "Are you okay?" Noah asked, concern roughening his voice.

I straightened up and rested my other foot on the ground. The moment I put any weight on it, a fresh throbbing woke up in my ankle. Shit.

Every nerve in my body recoiled against admitting this, but I couldn't exactly hide it. "I think I might have sprained it. But—it'll be fine. We'll just find a branch I can use as a sort of crutch. It's not like we were walking all that fast to begin with."

Of course, my good leg was going to tire out a whole lot faster if it was doing the brunt of the work. My muscles were already stiff from the past two nights of trekking.

I bit my lip, and Emeric took a cautious step closer. "If you'll let me—since I specialized in physicality, I got a few of the advanced lessons on healing. It's not my main area, so I'm not a medical professional by any means, but I should be able to make it a little better."

The thought of him putting his hands on me—and of the last time he'd put those hands on me for any extended time—sent an uneasy quiver down my spine. But the best

I'd be able to do was numb the joint, which even I knew would potentially make things worse in the long run if I wasn't aware that I was putting too much strain on the already bruised ligaments, and from Noah's silence he couldn't offer much more.

This was a matter of survival. If a freaking werewolf had come along and offered to fix me up, I'd have had to accept.

"All right. See what you can do." I glanced around and sank onto a broad tree root protruding from the ground nearby. "I guess we're lucky this is the first significant sprain any of us has gotten."

"The forest definitely isn't ideal for midnight rambles," Emeric said evenly. "I suppose we could switch to walking during the day and just keep more wards up."

I shook my head. "We're already draining our magic as it is." The fears of the forest critters were hardly enough to sustain the amount of casting I'd been doing in the past couple of days. The space behind my breastbone was starting to feel uncomfortably close to empty. "I could have tripped just as easily during the day anyway."

Emeric didn't argue, just knelt down by my outstretched leg. Noah positioned himself next to me as if he thought he might need to leap to my defense. The other guy lifted my foot with his titanium fingers carefully wrapped around my injured ankle—his prosthetic would probably keep it steadier than his regular hand. He'd stopped wearing his gloves in recognition of the summer heat and the lack of spectators, but the metal was warm against my skin.

He examined the joint gingerly with his other fingers. After a minute, he added a murmur of a casting here and there. A few tingling sensations traveled through my ankle. I couldn't determine how much they were actually doing. My leg didn't really hurt at all when I was resting it.

He was being awfully gentle about it. And thorough, as far as I could tell. My emotions tangled into a weird clash of feeling like I *should* be thankful but having trouble producing that sensation amid all the anger and hurt that still gnawed at me every time I looked at him. That emotional wound—the one he'd dealt me—ran a lot deeper than anything that'd happened to my ankle. It sure as hell wasn't going to be healed over with a few casting words.

After several attempts, Emeric frowned but appeared to decide that he'd done all he could. "I tried the strategies I used with my sister when she sprained her elbow a few years back. They at least helped stabilize the joint enough that it could heal faster. Test it out."

The reminder that Emeric had a sister—a sister he'd been trying to support by wheedling his way closer to the other reapers, rather than doing it all for selfish gain—dulled the discomfort of my inner wound just a little too. With Noah's help, I stood and then leaned my weight onto my injured ankle. The sharp throbbing had faded to a dull prickling. When I took a step, it deepened, but it was bearable.

"It's better," I said. "Still hurts a bit, but not too bad. Thank you."

Emeric dipped his head in acknowledgment. "It was the least I could do."

Well, technically the least he could have done was nothing at all, which might have suited him just fine not very long ago. But I held my tongue rather than point that out.

Noah made sure I was steady and then turned to peer through the forest. "We should still get you that crutch so you don't damage it more."

Emeric exhaled slowly. I could tell he didn't like what he was about to say before he even opened his mouth. "It was already going to be difficult making this hike with us in decent health. If we have to slow down more…"

I glowered at him. Surely he wasn't going to argue that the two of them should abandon me in the middle of the woods so I didn't slow them down. "What are you suggesting? If we had some other option, we'd have taken it already."

"That's not totally true." He paused, his gaze slipping away from me. "We've put a decent amount of distance between us and the Kingsleys' place. We've got the cover of night. I think it's time we take the risk of going out to the road and seeing if we can reach some kind of help from there."

CHAPTER NINE

Cressida

It turned out we'd come a lot farther from the road than I'd imagined. Either that, or the fact that I could only make limping progress, lurching along with the magic-warped branch-turned-crutch Noah had constructed for me, made it seem way farther than it actually was.

Thanks to Emeric's healing knowhow, I could put a little weight on my sprained ankle without feeling like I was worsening the injury, but that was still a far cry from walking normally. The dips and bumps in the forest floor —and all the debris that covered it—made for significantly harder travel when I had to worry about placing the crutch right too. Any time we came across a larger incline, Noah had to help me up with his hand on my arm.

Emeric was using some kind of spell to detect the

materials of the road, so at least we could be fairly sure we were heading in the right direction. But by the time he glanced over his shoulder to murmur, "We're almost there," my shoulder and armpit were aching from maneuvering the crutch, and my stomach was one tight ball of hunger.

Kato, who'd left Noah's shoulder after a doze to trundle through the wilderness alongside us, chittered demandingly from partway up one of the nearby trees. When Noah went over to him, the raccoon edged backward down the trunk. I understood why when he held out a paw to Noah, who triumphantly showed us an egg about half the size of a chicken's. "Omelets for breakfast, anyone?"

My lips twitched toward a smile despite my discomfort and growing exhaustion. Kato scrambled back up to grab another egg from the nest, while Emeric turned to watch with a frown.

"This isn't the best time for a scavenger hunt," he muttered. "The closer we get to the road, the more cautious we need to be. Stick together, no talking, nothing that could draw attention."

Noah gave him a smile that was noticeably tight around the edges. "I'm not in any hurry to end up back in chains, but I'd rather avoid starving too. Why don't you take the moment to scan for any signs of magic nearby?" His gaze slid to me, softening when it met mine. "I'd bet Cressida could use a short break."

"I'm fine," I said quickly, but the truth was I felt way too much relief as I sank down onto a log, stretching out my legs and rolling my shoulders. Emeric kept frowning, but he swiveled toward the road again and began speaking casting words under his breath.

Noah murmured a little magic of his own and then handed me the first of the eggs—now warm to the touch. "I think I managed to hard-boil it—or close enough. Better to eat it now than hold out for those omelets and risk it getting broken."

I would have insisted he eat the first one, but Kato was already scrambling back with more bounty, and the pang that shot through my gut couldn't be denied. I accepted the egg, willing my hand not to tremble with fatigue. "Thank you."

I peeled the eggshell off carefully and found the insides solidly rubbery. So far so good. I bit in and ended up gulping the whole thing down in a matter of seconds, barely tasting it, just wanting something more in my stomach.

In a few minutes, Noah had handed off an egg to Emeric and another to me, plus eaten at least one for himself. Kato ventured on to a different tree, so I guessed that nest was fully plundered. Emeric made a brisk gesture for us to get moving.

We tramped on as quietly as we could, even slower now. Every couple of minutes one of the guys stopped to speak a quick spell. The ground slanted upwards. Then, through the thinning trees, I made out a brighter fall of moonlight over the stretch of rural road.

Emeric walked the rest of the way to it. There, he stopped at the edge of the trees, cast another spell, and then pulled out his phone. He glanced up and down the road before returning to us with a grimace. "I'm getting a bar if I hold it high enough, but it's dropping in and out. There's a bit of a hill just south down the road. I think there's a decent chance I'll get enough of a signal to actually make a call there."

Noah nodded. We eased a little farther back into the brush and continued parallel with the road. By the time we made it up the hill, even my unsprained ankle was throbbing. I followed the guys as they walked within view of the road and then leaned against a tree trunk with a muffled sigh.

Emeric checked his phone again, the screen's glow casting his grim face in an eerie light, and exhaled in a rush. "Okay. First things first—we need to know where the hell we are."

As he tapped at his screen, Noah cast a spell checking for magic or approaching pursuers. A flicker of hope lit in my chest. This had been a pretty awful adventure, but we might be almost at the end of it. Once we got ahold of the barons and could tell them our location, surely they'd be able to send someone out to pick us up tomorrow? We'd just have to lay low and stay cautious for a little while longer—without all the tramping around.

Emeric had to pause and wave the phone around once, but it was only a minute or so before he was smiling— somberly, but I'd take it.

"Okay, it looks like we're about twenty miles from a small town called Jondale. That's the closest place that shows up on the map other than lakes in the middle of nowhere. Baron Killbrook and Baron Ashgrave gave me their phone numbers in case there was some problem and I needed to reach out to them. Who do you think is more likely to be up at three in the morning?"

Noah stepped toward him. "By now, they must know we're missing. I'd be surprised if my brother is sleeping at all. I'll talk to him." He held out his hand for the phone.

Emeric eyed him, his smile falling, as if he thought having a scion touch his device would contaminate it somehow. "I can handle a conversation."

Noah's voice took on a hint of an edge. "It's my brother. Let's get on with this."

Boys. Restraining a sigh and pushing myself forward, I shoved my hand into the mix. "*I'll* make the call, and then you won't have anything to argue about. What matters is getting out of here."

Both of the guys looked chagrinned. Emeric handed the phone over without further complaint, pointing out the name which simply said "Shauna school friend" in his Contacts list. Obviously he'd had to pretend he wouldn't want to spell out one of the "imposter" baron's names there in case one of his reaper allies looked at the phone.

The reminder of how he'd double-crossed us set my own teeth on edge, but I shook off that irritation and dialed the number. When I held the phone to my ear, the ringing sound crackled a little. The reception here was hardly *great.* I'd have to make this brief.

Declan Ashgrave picked up on the second ring, his tone urgent and alert as if Noah had been right about the no sleep thing. "Yes? Mr. Riplowe?"

"It's Cressida," I said quickly. "Well, we're all together. All three of us—Noah and Emeric and me." So much for brevity.

Before I could stumble over my words any more, Declan cut in. "Where are you? Are you all right? We sent someone out to Portland when Noah didn't check in—"

The connection hissed, and I lost his next few words. My pulse jumped with a renewed sense of urgency. "We're —we're pretty much okay, but we're stuck in the woods without a car, and some major reaper families are hunting for us. Could someone come pick us up?"

There must have been more static between us, drowning out some of my explanation. "What was that about a car?" Declan said.

"We don't have one," I said, as loud as I dared. "We need someone to come get us."

"Right, of course. Let me know where you are and I'll make arrangements right away."

He sounded as if he figured he could have someone to us in no time at all, three in the morning or not. I swallowed hard, the hope in my chest expanding. "The closest town is called Jondale. But we're in the woods north of there. If you can come up the road—"

"Sorry, you're in Jondale?" Declan said something else, but his voice was eaten by the fracturing connection.

"No, we're north of there, by the road that—"

Static fizzed in my ear, and then the call dropped completely. "Shit," I muttered, tapping the screen to call again, but instead I got an error message. The bar we'd had before had vanished.

My heart thudding, I waved the phone in the air and limped a few steps in one direction and then another, but the bar only returned for a second, dropping away as soon as I lowered my hand. The battery power was dwindling too. It wasn't as if Emeric had gotten any chance to charge it out here.

I swore again and glanced around, wondering if there was an even higher piece of land nearby we could try. Emeric took the phone from me and checked the screen. "Even if you didn't get all the information out, they should still have a decent idea where we are from that."

"I don't know if he heard the last thing I said at all. He thought I was saying we were *in* Jondale." My hands clenched. Stupid phone. Stupid reception. Stupid everything about this horrible situation.

"At least now they know approximately where we are and that we need help," Noah said. "If they don't find us in town, they'll spread out the search."

"But how long will it take them to get up here? Can we really afford to wait around—"

My mouth snapped shut, and my heart lurched at the faint sound my ears had just barely picked up. "Is that an engine?"

Even if I'd managed to tell Declan our exact location, no one from the barons could have gotten to us that quickly. And the rumble was already getting louder, heading toward us from farther up the road. From the north, in the direction of the chalet.

Emeric spat out a quick casting word and stiffened. "There's a searching spell moving through the forest from that direction too. Come on! We have to try to get out of range."

Noah's head jerked toward me. Without stopping to ask, he swept me up, tucked me against his lean back piggyback style, and dashed forward into the deeper woods carrying me. My arms whipped around his shoulders instinctively, my body swaying with the erratic rhythm of his strides across the forest floor. I might have protested if I hadn't known how important it was that we move quickly—and how incapable I was of doing that at the moment.

Emeric jogged alongside us, clutching the straps of his backpack, his jaw tight. In a ragged voice, he intoned a few words that I assumed were some kind of spell he hoped would at least temporarily deflect the one rippling toward us.

How deep into the forest would the searching spell reach? The mage casting it would have to keep propelling it out with the movement of the car—they wouldn't have time to stretch it too far, I didn't think. But then, we weren't likely to be able to run all that far in the time it'd take the car to catch up with our former position, even with Noah hauling my ass.

His breath was already coming short. He'd been putting on an upbeat front all this time, but he had to be tired and hungry too. I wished I could do more than cling to him like some invalid.

The sound of the engine had petered away in the distance. I glanced over my shoulder, but couldn't make out any light through the trees. Emeric tossed out another casting word and another, his voice getting hoarse with the exertion of the run.

It felt as if we'd been hurtling through the brush for several minutes when he finally raised his hand for us to stop. "The car's passed us. It hasn't stopped—still moving away. I don't think they picked up on our presence."

Noah swayed on his feet, and I squirmed so he let me drop—gently—to the ground. He looked at me with an apologetic twist of his lips.

I touched his arm briefly. "It's okay. You did what made sense to get us out of there safely." I paused and managed to put on an almost light-hearted tone. "Now you just owe me a new crutch."

"That I can do," he said, but there wasn't much humor in his voice either.

Now we knew how closely the reapers were watching the road. If we hadn't heard the engine as soon as we had —if we hadn't been able to move as quickly…

I let out my breath in a rush. "And I *am* going to need that crutch, because clearly our best option is to keep on hiking those last twenty miles to Jondale. And if we're lucky, we'll find a welcoming party there waiting to whisk us home."

Although given how our luck had gone so far, I wasn't going to count on it.

CHAPTER TEN

Cressida

Something was chasing me. I kept darting glances behind me as I stumbled through the woods, but I couldn't make out more than a blur. I just knew that if it caught me, it would sink vicious claws into my skin, snap brutal jaws around my neck, and wrench me apart in the most painful possible way. Then it roared, a booming guttural sound that—

That snapped me out of my nightmare into one much more real if less immediately terrifying.

I was lying on a mat of leaves with a blanket formed out of more leaves draped over me and a small stick structure arching over my head to block out the sun. It *had* been sunny when I'd set my head down this morning. Now the light around me was dim and gray.

And another booming sound crackled through the air. Not the roar of an imaginary monster—thunder. Humid air wafted against my face. The dim light flickered with what must have been a lightning flash.

Every part of me ached from my feet to my head, which felt as muggy as the air. I wanted nothing more than to roll over and cling to sleep a little longer. But before I could do anything other than think about that, raindrops began to patter against my blanket of leaves. A few fat ones slipped past the sun shade to splat against my neck and jaw.

With a groan, I shoved myself into a sitting position—just as the clouds overhead opened up completely.

A torrent that felt more like a waterfall than rain washed over me, drenching me to the bone in an instant. A yelp escaped my throat. I jumped up, swiping stray locks of hair out of my eyes.

The vague forms of Noah and Emeric moved in the deluge around me, sputtering casting words. The shock of the water woke me up enough to give me the wherewithal to pitch in.

Murmuring a casting word, I imagined a barrier of solid air arcing over us, matching my intention to the tingling energy I could feel that the guys had already constructed. The space behind my sternum ached too, but not from muscle strain. I was just about running on empty.

Steeling myself, I tore a few more shreds of magic out of me, adding to our invisible shelter. The guys had to be just as drained as I was. If we didn't all give it whatever we had, we weren't going to make much of anything.

The downpour eased off on me and then totally

abated, water streaking over the transparent dome we'd created that covered the three of us standing just a few feet apart and not much else. The rain cascaded over the edges of our shelter to drum against the ground in a ring that looked even more like a waterfall, soaking into the earth.

I rubbed my arms, slick with moisture I had no way of drying off. At least the temperature was still summer-warm, so I wasn't going to get a chill, but my sopping hair and dress weren't exactly comfortable for standing around either.

Noah ran his fingers through his own sodden hair, pushing it back from his face, and aimed another casting word at a crack that formed in our dome. The dribbling of water that'd started to seep through stopped.

Emeric muttered to himself with words that didn't sound magical at all as he checked over his dripping backpack. I caught a tremor of dismay from Percy, who was hunched in the partial shelter of a thick branch somewhere nearby.

"Well," I said, squeezing as much of the water from my braid as I could, "what's August without a thunderstorm or two? I guess we have to just wait this out and—"

Another bellow of thunder cut me off, and the rain battered our magical barrier even harder. I might have been worried about it fracturing if an even more pressing worry hadn't risen up right then: a wash of water rippling over the ground toward our feet, carrying leaves and chunks of dirt with it.

Emeric spotted the flood at the same time and

outright swore. "The stream must have overflowed. Come on, we've got to find higher ground. Pull the shelter along as well as you can."

The flood was already coursing around my sneakers. I hurried along with the guys, my shoes squishing unpleasantly with each step, my ankle soon twinging. It was feeling better after the rest, but I'd left my crutch behind somewhere in that watery mess. Hopefully I didn't need it that badly now.

The air overhead shivered, and a smattering of rain broke through. I tossed another casting word at it with a deeper pang in my chest. Noah did the same, catching my elbow to offer extra support.

We hustled on between the trees, following Emeric, who'd taken the lead. He was striding along as if he had some idea where he was going. Here was hoping he wasn't faking that like he had so much else.

When the dome shuddered again, I couldn't summon the energy to shore it up. Any wild creatures we might have frightened during a typical walk must be too busy hiding from the rain to pay any attention to us right now, so nothing was replenishing my stores of magic.

Emeric snapped at the barrier, but it wasn't enough. A second later, the shield of solid air splintered apart, opening us to the full force of the storm again.

All of us cursing now, we waded through the deluge. Even blinking hard, I could barely make out anything beyond Emeric's blurred form ahead of me. But I felt it when the ground slanted upward. We pushed on through the brush, the prickly branches of a shrub scratching my calves, and the water that had been licking at my sneakers eased back.

The downpour eased up just a bit, and Emeric let out a little shout that sounded more encouraging than dismayed. As Noah and I caught up with him on what turned out to be a low ridge in the forest, he pointed down the other side. Through a sparser stretch of trees, I spotted a form that looked like a cabin.

My heart leapt with a mix of excitement and nerves. Who knew who the hell we'd run into there? But I'd be willing to face just about anyone to get out of this rain.

With unspoken agreement, we all headed down the other side of the ridge, skidding here and there on the increasingly muddy ground. Noah clipped his shoulder on a tree with a wince. Then we were stumbling into an overgrown clearing around the log cabin, which had a rusty pick-up truck parked outside, its windshield cracked.

The cabin wasn't in any better shape. Its door was gone, leaving only empty hinges. We tramped into what turned out to be a single room, letting out a collective sigh as soon as the rain was off us.

There was obviously no one here now, and it didn't look as if anyone had lived in this place for quite a while. A single bedframe without even a mattress squatted in one corner. Noah ran his finger through a thick layer of dust on the small table that had lost its chair, if it'd ever had one. The door had also been taken off the old white fridge in the small kitchen area. Emeric tried the tiny sink, which sputtered and groaned but didn't emit any more than a brief spray.

I jabbed my thumb toward the doorway. "If we want water, there's plenty out there." At least we could stay dry in here without having to expend any magic. Or rather, not continue to be drenched. A puddle was already forming under my feet from my sopping clothes. At this particular moment, it was hard to imagine ever feeling *dry* again.

Looking on the bright side, I was a heck of a lot cleaner than I'd been half an hour ago. The unexpected shower had washed the grime from my skin and my dress.

I ran my hands over the thin fabric, trying to push more of the moisture out of it, and Noah's gaze tracked the movement. Glancing at him, seeing the spark of heat in his eyes, I became abruptly aware of how tightly the wet dress was clinging to the curves of my body. The edges of my bra and panties were clearly visible, starker than the other wrinkles.

Noah jerked his gaze away, but a little heat of my own had kindled in my chest at his glance. My body wasn't the only one on display. Noah's T-shirt was plastered to the lean muscles I'd enjoyed running my hands over so much on that night that should have never happened, and Emeric's brawn—

I cut off that thought and the direction of my gaze, glaring at the floor instead. I sure as hell wasn't going to stand here admiring *that* jerk's musculature, as impressive as it might be.

I moved to the bedframe and sank down onto the edge, which might be dusty but at least didn't have any puddles streaking across it like the floor did. We were out of the rain, but I wasn't sure we were going to get much more rest. My stomach gurgled, as much nausea as hunger, and my throat pinched. For all the water around us, I hadn't had a drink since I'd woken up.

I scrambled back to my feet. "We should put the water bottles out to fill up while it's raining. That water will be cleaner than anything we've been able to collect so far." I wasn't sure whether it was our recent poor eating habits or the stream water that was contributing to the faint nausea that had been developing in my gut since last night, but a better source couldn't hurt.

Emeric headed over to the doorway, pulling the bottles out of his pack as he went. "I can conjure a sort of funnel to make sure plenty of water goes in. It won't take long." He paused. "We have those mushrooms the raccoon gathered that we haven't eaten yet, if we trust the familiar to know what it's doing?"

The raccoon in question came trundling into the cabin a moment later, wet and bedraggled. Kato grunted and curled up on the floor next to Noah's feet. He grinned crookedly and held out his hand. "I think he's a good judge of what's edible. Might as well get cooking while there's not much else we can do."

As Emeric set up the water bottles with his funnel spell, Noah found a dusty dinner plate in one of the kitchen cupboards and conjured his magical fire on that so he wasn't risking burning the whole cabin down. He dug a rusty frying pan out of a drawer, held it out in the rain to wash it and gather a little water, and in a few minutes we had chunks of mottled white-and-brown mushroom sizzling in a very weak stew.

Emeric threw in a few more bits of wild garlic he had on hand. I could tell my standards were getting very low, because after that the smell was enough to make my mouth water.

We ate a quick dinner of mushroom garlic stew and fresh rainwater. It wasn't a lot, but when I'd gulped all of mine down out of one of the stones Emeric had shaped with magic into bowls a couple of days ago, my queasiness retreated and my head felt… maybe not clear, but at least less muggy.

I glanced toward the doorway, where the thunderstorm had dwindled into a softer rain. The drops made a pinging sound off the hood and roof of the pick-up truck.

I lifted my chin toward it. "Do you think there's any chance we could get that thing running?" Now that the downpour had thinned, I could make out a narrow lane choked with weeds that must lead to the main road. It wouldn't be an easy drive, but once we were on the main road, all we'd have to do was zip into Jondale before the reapers did another sweep of the area.

Emeric's face lit up so suddenly my heart skipped a beat. He *was* a pretty good-looking guy when he wasn't scowling—I mean, if you ignored the whole screwing over your supposed allies thing, which I wasn't going to.

"I can take a look," he said. "I did some engine work back in Portland."

"Kind of a jack of all trades, huh?" Noah said with vague amusement.

Emeric's expression darkened with a glower he aimed at the scion. "*Some* of us need to do whatever we can to make ends meet. But mechanical work is more my strong point than healing. Anything that runs on oil or gas or both… There's kind of an art to it that I happen to like." His gaze darted to me for a second, and the memory rose up of the night he'd taken me out to the ocean and sculpted figures out of the water to show off his skills.

The night we'd first kissed.

I guessed his enthusiasm for working with liquid materials hadn't been a lie, but a burn that was as much embarrassment as anything else crept into my cheeks.

Emeric jerked his gaze away. "Whether it'll work depends on how far gone the engine is." He looked down at his hands, flexing both the one of flesh and the titanium one. "I'm getting pretty low on juice, though. We'll want to wait for it to stop raining before I open up the hood anyway. I'll go out there now and see if I can find some of wildlife to startle, replenish the stock."

Noah rubbed his own hands together. "That's not a bad idea for all of us."

It wasn't, as much as I hated the thought of going back out into the rain. My clothes had only just reached the point where I could call them damp instead of drenched. But I hated feeling drained and powerless even more.

By the time I'd dragged myself out of the cabin, the rain had slowed even more, really just a drizzle now. Which was good for other reasons too, because birds were starting to twitter in the trees. We had some wildlife to scare.

We set off in different directions. I grabbed a stick to smack tree trunks and shrubs, and mentally urged Percy to see if he could find some doves or voles to terrify, since any fear my familiar stirred up would pass on to me. If he caught them afterward and could spare us a few to snack on, so much the better.

When I'd cycled back around, only sparse glimmers of magic shifted in my chest, but it was more than I'd had before. The rain had let up completely.

Emeric had the truck's hood propped open. He leaned over the engine, his mouth set in a tight line of concentration.

"It doesn't look good," he said. "It's been here a while. Not much gas in the tank either. But if I can jumpstart the engine, it might be enough to get us the short distance to town."

Noah came up beside him. "Let me know if there's anything I can do to help."

Emeric eyed him narrowly like he had when Noah had asked for his phone last night. "I think I can manage on my own, thanks."

I rolled my eyes but didn't comment. Emeric muttered one word and then another, and nothing he did appeared to work. He probably didn't enjoy having the two of us as an audience, but it wasn't as if we had much else to do.

After several tries, something he said brought a faint whirring sound out of the engine. My heart leapt. "Is it—"

The sound faded away before I could even finish the

question, but a hint of a smile curled Emeric's lips. "We're getting there. If I tweak it just a little…"

As he drew in a breath to speak another casting word, Noah flinched. He spun toward the ridge we'd clambered over and then back toward us. "Someone's coming."

Emeric snapped upright, nearly banging his head on the hood. "What?"

"I never took down my wards around our last campsite, we got out of there so fast. One of them just pinged me—another spell touched it. Which means whoever cast that spell has to be close."

"Damn it." Emeric glared at the engine for a second, maybe debating whether he could get the truck running in time for us to make a run for it on wheels. My pulse had sped up to twice its usual pace.

I took a wobbly step in the opposite direction. "There isn't time. If they noticed our wards, they'll be coming fast." Maybe the truck wouldn't have worked anyway, no matter how much time Emeric had.

As if proving my words, a mild prickling sensation raced over my skin. My nerves jumped at the same time as both of the guys stiffened. It was some kind of searching spell, and it'd just found not only our wards but *us*.

"Let's go!" Noah demanded in a hushed voice, and tugged me toward the woods beyond the cabin. We all knew that if a searching spell could reach us from wherever our pursuers were, there were plenty of more violent spells they could send after us too.

With a grimace, Emeric wrenched himself away from the truck. We dashed into the thicker forest in a frantic rush that was becoming uncomfortably familiar. Even with my ankle still a little sore, I was getting a lot better at setting my feet on the most stable spots, veering around bushes at just the right moment not to have to slow down too much.

A wave of hissing energy whipped through the trees toward us. I threw myself forward even faster, gritting my teeth against a sharper pang in my ankle, but it was worth it. The spell petered out just behind me, the slightest lick of it catching my heel—and numbing the skin there.

If it'd hit us properly, we'd have been paralyzed.

We hurtled onward, our breaths rasping, our feet squelching in the mud. Noah swerved a little to the left once and then again, presumably hoping to get out of the path of the reapers' spells.

In my panic, a bolt of brilliance hit me. With my new stores of magic, I called out a casting word and tossed it back the way we'd come.

An illusion. It was shaky because I'd been so hasty with it, but that shouldn't matter through the trees. The reapers would see three figures that looked somewhat like us darting through the forest in the other direction, heading closer to the road.

We couldn't count on it distracting them for long, though. We needed as much distance from them as we could get. From Emeric's muttering, he was casting more spells around us to muffle the sounds of our passage.

We hurried onward. The light around us dwindled with the coming dusk. My lungs and my calves burned from the exertion. We were running on pure adrenaline, nothing but the instinct to survive. My legs were starting to sway under me, but every time I considered stopping, I pushed myself forward again.

Just one more minute. Just one more minute. The farther we went, the more likely they wouldn't find us when we finally did have to rest.

Emeric eased up on his pace first, what felt like hours later. There'd been no sign of pursuit since the dusk had fallen. He glanced over at Noah and me, looking as if he was about to speak—and at the same moment, Noah lurched to a halt with a horrible, rasping clang. He fell face-first into the brush, a strangled sound escaping him that was all pain.

I sprang to his side and froze, my breath stopping. A large metal trap had clamped its jaws around his leg.

CHAPTER ELEVEN

Cressida

"Don't move!" Emeric said to Noah, low but urgent. From the noise Noah made, I wasn't sure he was even capable of moving if he'd wanted to.

My gut twisted. I wanted to wrench that awful thing off his leg and hurl it away from here, but I had no idea how to do that without hurting him even worse.

Emeric knelt beside him, his entire body tensed. Remembering how he'd reacted to Noah in the past, I wondered if he even really wanted to help the other guy. He obviously saw the scions who'd turned against the old barons as even worse than people like me who'd simply changed sides once the rebellion was already underway.

My fingers twitched, but if I stopped him from doing whatever he could, there was no one else here who'd be able to fix this.

Instead, I stumbled over to crouch by Noah's head.

He'd turned his face to the side, his eyes closed and his mouth twisted, dirt speckling his cheek. Not knowing what else to do, I grasped his hand and squeezed it with as much reassurance as I could offer.

Emeric murmured a couple of casting words as he examined the trap, but the pain etched on Noah's face didn't soften at all. The former reaper swiped the heel of his hand across his forehead. "It must be some kind of bear trap. Old—someone forgot it out here. The mechanism is rusted, so I don't think it closed as hard or as deep as it could have, but it's still pretty brutal."

"Just get it off him!" I snapped.

Emeric's gaze flicked to me, his own voice sharpening. "I will as soon as I'm sure of how to without breaking anything that's not already broken."

Even in the dusk, I could tell that the trap's teeth had sunk right through Noah's jeans into his leg. Dark patches of blood mottled the fabric. Hopefully Emeric had at least slowed down the bleeding.

Noah's breath still came with a pained rasp, but he opened his eyes. "Do whatever you need to," he said hoarsely. His grip on my hand tightened. All my innards seemed to have tangled into one huge knot.

He wouldn't be here in this horrible situation at all if it hadn't been for me.

Emeric inhaled slowly and spoke one careful casting word and then another. He touched the trap's jaws, and they eased apart. A fresh spurt of blood flowed up from the vicious wound, and I jerked my eyes away with a heave of my stomach.

"I don't know if I can handle this with magic alone," Emeric said. "See if you can find some moss."

Moss. I let go of Noah's hand reluctantly and spun around, peering through the shadowed forest with a new sense of purpose to keep me going.

I hustled toward a log I spotted, which didn't offer much, but a boulder near it had several chunks I managed to pry off. Clutching my findings against my chest, I hurried back. My own ankle was throbbing after our run, but I ignored it. I doubted it hurt even a tenth as badly as Noah's leg did right now.

When I made it back to the guys, Emeric had cut off the leg of Noah's jeans just below the knee. I thrust my bounty at him, and he grabbed the pieces. While he pressed them to the puncture wounds, he tied the cut fabric around them in a tight bandage. With a few more casting words, he sat back on his heels, looking satisfied if not exactly pleased.

And incredibly weary. How much magic did *he* have left after all that?

"That should have stabilized the bleeding," he said. "I don't know how often we'd be supposed to change the moss or whatever—it's just something I heard about in some book. My mom was kind of big into backwoods stuff." The mom who'd abandoned his family. He wiped at his face again, leaving a smear of mud. "I'd guess the bigger concern will be infection. And keeping moving. You're not walking far like that."

Noah eased himself up on his arms tentatively and then turned so he was sitting. His face was sallower than usual with sweat beaded on his forehead, but at least he didn't look outright agonized anymore.

"We'll carry him if we have to," I said firmly.

Noah grimaced and shook his head. "I'll manage. I'm not slowing you two down." He managed a weak laugh. "It can't be too much farther to town after that last run."

"I don't know," Emeric muttered. "We weren't exactly following the most straightforward route. I'm not sure how far off-track we might have gotten. And I don't think you're going to have much choice when it comes to going slow. If you wanted to pull your weight, you should have been watching where you were putting your feet."

Noah's gaze cut to the other guy. "As you just pointed out, we were running for our *lives*, not taking a casual stroll with a carefully calculated route. It's not as if I wanted to step on that thing."

"But you did, and now we have to live with the consequences." Emeric sighed and pushed himself to standing. "I'd better make sure the reapers don't descend on us while you're recuperating here, and I need to shore up my magic for that."

"I can cast a few wards," Noah said tersely.

I sprang to my feet. Emeric's attitude was grating on my nerves—and reminding me that it *wasn't* my fault any of us were in this situation. If Noah and I had continued our lives as we'd expected, we'd both be back at Blood U right now, attending classes and awkwardly avoiding the subject of our illicit hook-up.

No, Emeric had just *had* to barge into our lives and drag us into his awful plot to ruin me and the new barons.

He had gotten us taken to the chalet, and *his* shoddy escape plan had landed us in the woods with nothing to carry us toward safety but our feet. And now he was going to snark at Noah for getting horribly hurt, as if he'd done it on purpose to inconvenience us?

The words seared over my tongue. "You're the last person who should be shooting your mouth off about supposedly bad decisions. There are totally understandable mistakes and then there's going out of your way to screw people over, and we all know who the champion of the second one is here."

Emeric flinched, but his jaw clenched at the same time. "I healed him, didn't I? I've been doing everything I can to make up for my screw-ups. And they *were* mistakes —I had the wrong idea—I'm not the kind of person who'd want to see someone tormented just for the fun of it."

"Oh, no?" I set my hands on my hips. "It seems like you must have been having plenty of fun watching me blunder around unknowing. We'd spent plenty of time together before the worst of what happened to me in Portland, and I can't think of a single thing I said or did that should have made you feel justified. But you went ahead with the torture anyway, didn't you?"

"It's not that easy when you're locked in—and I figured you were putting on a front."

"Of course, because acting like someone you're not came so easily to *you*, so why wouldn't everyone else be doing it too?"

"Guys," Noah said pleadingly, but my temper was too

close to boiling for me to simmer down now, and it appeared to be the same with Emeric.

"The only thing I've ever lied to you about was the real reason I wanted you to come to Portland," he retorted, his pale eyes flashing. "And there were a few things I decided simply not to bring up. When I realized I'd had the wrong idea about you, I tried to stop all of this from happening."

"Well, that came too little too late. And after you humiliated me all by yourself for no one's gain but your own." The memory of him pushing away from me on the bed and hustling out of the room, leaving me disheveled and half-undressed, came back to me with a flare of heat that was shame as well as anger. How had I managed to miss what a *jerk* he was?

Emeric glowered back at me. "I didn't force anything on you. You seemed perfectly happy to jump into bed with a guy you'd hardly known two weeks."

"Hey," Noah cut in again, his tone sharper now. His face had flushed too, and I realized he hadn't known how close Emeric and I had come to sleeping together. I hadn't wanted to risk him getting jealous when I wasn't sure anything was going to happen between Emeric and me anyway, and afterward I'd been so embarrassed by the rejection…

But if Noah was upset about that, he didn't seem to blame me for it. "You're lucky Cressida ever gave you the time of day," he went on. "Don't attack her just because she can't get over everything you did to hurt her in an instant."

"It's been a hell of a lot more than an instant." Emeric

jerked his hand through the air. "For *days*, I've been pushing myself as hard as I can, using every shred of magic I have getting the two of you back to your vaunted university."

A sudden, chilling thought gripped me. "*Have* you? Because… we hadn't seen a hint of the reapers since we first got away from them until *you* insisted on going closer to the road. And you were the one who pointed out that cabin. How do we know you weren't signaling them somehow, bringing them down on us?"

For a second, Emeric just gaped at me, speechless. "Are you kidding me?" he sputtered.

Noah's eyes had narrowed. "You did insist on going off in the woods on your own before you started working on the truck—before they showed up today. And it's pretty convenient for the reapers that *your* phone cut out just before Cressida could tell my brother exactly where we are."

Emeric glared back at him. "Why would I go to all the trouble of breaking you out of the Kingsleys' house just to toss you back to them? They were a lot happier with me before I did that."

"I don't know," I said. "Maybe you've gotten tired of 'pushing' yourself, and you figure you're better off handing us over and hoping you can get on their good side again. Maybe this is all part of some new, elaborate scheme to try to get information out of us while we're stuck out here alone."

Something in Emeric deflated. His shoulders slumped, the fury fading from his face. "It *isn't*," he said emphatically. "I fucked up. Epically. And I know it. I put you through a ton of crap that you didn't deserve, and I'm trying my best to get you out of it. All I want right now is to help you. That's all I've *been* doing since you ended up at the Kingsleys'. Why can't you believe that?"

The threat of hopelessness in his voice dampened my own anger. I swallowed hard, searching for an answer. "When you've fucked up that epically, of course it's going to take a hell of a lot to prove you're not going to do it again."

He spread his hands in a gesture of surrender. "Fine. I get that. What's it going to take to prove it, then? What can I do so that you'll trust me enough that you're not assuming I'm out to hurt you all over again every time anything goes a little wrong? Because at this point, I don't think we're getting out of these woods safely if we're at each other's throats like this."

I hesitated. My stomach was roiling, all my nerves stripped raw from the argument. When I tried to imagine a scenario where I accepted Emeric's help as easily as I had before I'd found out how horribly he'd betrayed us, nothing came to me.

"Maybe there isn't anything you can do," I said quietly. "Maybe you should go find your own route home and throw yourself on the reapers' mercy or the barons, whichever you prefer—although I've got to tell you, I think the barons are a much safer bet—and Noah and I will figure out how we're going to get back just the two of us."

Emeric's stance went totally rigid. A flicker of fear washed from him into me. "You mean that?"

Even the anxiety he felt over the idea of us casting him off wasn't enough to convince me. He could simply be scared that he'd lose his chance to finish whatever other plans he might have made with the reapers.

Noah rubbed his face, looking as exhausted by the conversation as I was. "I'll stand by whatever Cressida decides. We don't have that much farther to go. We have our magic and our familiars. It might be better if we don't have to worry about your motivations on top of surviving."

The fact that even the ever-optimistic scion was ready to throw in the towel on getting along sent a pang through my chest, but not a big enough one to change my mind. I just kept watching Emeric, studying his response.

The muscle in his jaw ticked with a tightening of his mouth. He pulled his gaze away from me, casting it around as if searching for something that would turn this standoff around. Then he bent down and grabbed a few stones within reach.

I stared, puzzled, as he hurled them one by one in different directions into the woods. The rustling and flapping of disturbed animals clued me in—he was gathering fear to fuel his magic. For what? I braced myself, my hands balling at my sides.

But Emeric didn't aim any spell our way. He simply raised his titanium hand, gleaming faintly in the dimming light, and met my eyes again. There was something wild, even a little unsettling, in his gaze. His voice came out with a thrum of magic that I immediately knew was binding him to the words he said.

"I swear to protect and support Cressida Warbury and Noah Ashgrave in every way I can, from the procuring of food and water to defense from those who wish to capture us and the overcoming of any other obstacle we face, until we reach Bloodstone University. If I deviate from that promise in any way, if there is the slightest thing that I could do to help them survive the trip that I refuse to do, let me shatter my own skull with this hand."

My heart lurched. "Emeric." He hadn't even added any caveats to shield himself.

If he broke from that oath, I had no doubt his titanium hand could break his skull as he'd said, killing him in the process. But to see his promise through, he might very well end up risking his life at the hands of the reapers or whatever else we might face out here instead.

He'd put his own survival quite literally on the line to guarantee ours.

Noah had fallen into shocked silence. Emeric lowered his hand, the quiver of magic in the air dissipating, his mouth set in a grim line. And I realized that the one thing his oath didn't prevent was me still telling him to take off. If I insisted that the best way he could support us was to strike out on his own—and I could make a case for that— he'd have to leave despite what he'd just sworn to.

"Why would you do that?" I asked. I couldn't imagine taking an oath like that for anyone. Even the joint magical promise I'd entered with Rory when we were still at odds had benefitted me as much as her—and put me under threat of nothing more than a little disapproval—and I'd struggled to convince myself to agree to that.

"I fucked up," Emeric said, his voice steady if rough. "I didn't recognize what really mattered. Not a single one of those bastards chasing us matters a fraction as much to me as you do. You're worth a hundred of any of them. So I'm in this, whether you believe me or not, whether you trust me or not. That oath is the clearest way I have of showing it."

I didn't know what I'd done to deserve that kind of devotion, but I couldn't exactly argue with it either. I wavered on my feet and glanced at Noah. He looked up at me from where he was resting his wounded leg and gave a hint of a shrug, as if to say it was up to me. I could tell from his expression that he recognized just how huge Emeric's promise had been too.

It didn't change all that much. It didn't mean I was going to trust him whole-heartedly. But... I couldn't summon any of the anger or resignation I'd felt before, that had made separating seem like the only viable option.

What he'd offered hadn't changed much, but it'd changed enough.

The intensity in his eyes sent a weird heat wavering over my skin and through my chest. "All right," I said, turning away from him. "We're better off pooling our resources anyway, if we have the guarantee that you're not going to call in the reapers on us. So, what do we do now?"

CHAPTER TWELVE

Noah

As I emerged from sleep, the pain rippled up from my calf in waves. Emeric had cast another numbing spell on it a couple of hours ago when we'd set up camp, and I didn't like how quickly its effect had faded. The last thing I wanted was to be constantly calling on him for help.

I shifted on my bed of leaves, careful not to move that leg any more than I had to, and murmured a spell of my own. Numbing was basic first aid—we all learned it in the first year of our magical studies. But my magic was pretty drained. I didn't want to risk going completely dry when we had no idea how much distance we'd actually put between us and our pursuers.

The pain only dulled a little. It was enough relief for me to doze off into another hazy stretch of sleep, but every crackle and rustle in the forest hit me with a jolt of adrenaline. After the thunderstorm had interrupted our daytime rest, we'd decided to spend some of tonight recuperating, but I wasn't managing to accomplish much of that, as hard as I'd been trying.

The reapers had almost caught us. I was practically crippled now until we could reach someone who knew a full range of healing techniques. I had to stay sharp, had to be at my best in every other possible way until then.

Unfortunately, knowing that only made it harder to wind down.

The rain had washed away a lot of the summer heat, and the temperature had dropped even more overnight. In my still slightly damp clothes, the brush of the breeze felt almost chilly. I debated scavenging for more fallen leaves to thicken my makeshift blanket, but the thought only made me feel more tired. So I just drifted a little more in my uncomfortable state until I got too restless to keep trying.

I sat up carefully and quietly, with a soft casting word to check that the wards we'd set up around our camp were still active. Then I glanced around the spot. Cressida and Emeric were sprawled under their own blankets of leaves, Cressida's pulled all the way to her ears. Her pale braid, which she'd painstakingly rewoven last night, poked out from beneath.

As I watched, a shiver ran through her form, and she curled her knees up higher under the leaves. My chest constricted. She was cold too.

If things had been normal between us, if I could have touched her without worrying that it'd be a reminder of some of the worst times in her life, I'd have gone over and wrapped my arms around her, sharing my warmth. But as much as I ached to do that, I suspected it wouldn't actually comfort her in the long run. Instead, I murmured a thin wash of heated air over her body to take the edge off the chill.

It looked as if she relaxed a little. At least I'd helped somehow or other.

My own arms were breaking out in goosebumps now that I'd shed my blanket. The abrupt change in temperature had left my muscles even stiffer than usual.

I had no clothes except what I was wearing, and I didn't like the idea of conjuring a fire at night when the light might show at a distance. But if I was going to be up anyway, I could find some way of contributing. Besides, I needed to practice moving around with this injury.

I scooted over to a nearby tree and used the trunk for leverage to heave myself onto my feet. Well, foot, since one brush of the other one against the ground sent a sharper surge of pain through my leg. So… I guessed I was resorting to hopping?

As I grimaced, Kato scurried through the brush to me in a similarly lopsided way. He deposited a small egg on a patch of leaves—next to a couple of others he must have already brought. When he glanced up at me with a quiet chitter, I smiled at him and sent a flicker of gratitude through my bond. *Good job. Keep it up. We need all the nourishment we can get.*

He couldn't hear those exact words from me, of course, but I knew he got the general idea. As he trotted off into the shadows again, a weird twist of jealousy clutched my gut.

My familiar was doing more to keep us alive than I was right now. If I hadn't stepped on that stupid trap—

I closed my eyes and took one slow breath and another. There was no way of turning back time. I had to make the best of the situation I was in *now*, not stress over what could have been. That's what Declan would have said.

Of course, somehow I suspected my older brother would have managed not to stomp on a bear trap in the first place.

At least I could assume he'd be so relieved to have me back safe and sound that he wouldn't fuss too much about exactly how well or not I'd handled myself during this adventure. Not that he was ever cruel in his judgments— he just couldn't help analyzing situations from his own, highly practical and experienced perspective.

I did have a little experience with adapting to leg injuries now, even if Cressida's hadn't been half as bad as mine. Bracing my hand against the tree, I hopped over to a fallen branch and shaped it into a crutch of my own with a few minutes' concentration and a grating sensation deep in my chest where I was scraping the bottom of the barrel when it came to my magic. Somewhere to my right, Kato startled a couple of smaller creatures scuttling around, sending a welcome quiver of fear my way.

Cressida had been able to use her weaker foot for balance while she'd been recovering from her sprain. I quickly determined that the second I added any weight at all to my wounded leg, it set off a spike of agony so intense I had to bite back a gasp. So I was still stuck with hopping, but the crutch did help me keep my balance.

It took way too much effort to venture just a short distance into the woods, scanning the forest floor and the foliage around me. I did manage to spot a couple of the kind of mushrooms Kato had scrounged up for us before and that we'd eaten without any ill effects, so I bent to grab those.

In doing so, I threw myself completely off and ended up toppling onto my ass.

Pain seared from my wound. I clamped my mouth shut against any noise that might wake up the others if my fall hadn't already, but something like a whimper managed to escape me anyway. Clenching my jaw, I willed back the sensation until my breath was no longer hitching. Then I plucked the damned mushrooms and hauled myself upright again.

Maybe I'd been a little optimistic thinking I wouldn't slow us down that much. Fuck.

As I swayed back to the campsite, an idea wavered up through my mind. I didn't *have* to slow them down. I could tell them to leave me here with Kato, and my familiar would make sure I didn't starve. They'd reach town so much faster and then they could send back help for me.

I glanced at Cressida's sleeping form, and my throat tightened. I didn't *want* to see her leave—especially with the jerk who'd already cost her so much, whatever promises he'd made yesterday.

But… what if that was the kindest thing I could do for her?

In the time it'd taken me to retrieve those two mushrooms, Kato had brought back four more eggs and a few mushrooms of his own. I mock-glowered at him and then gave his back a good scratch. "Good job, *mon pote*. We'll take anything else you can find."

Cressida might have been asleep, but her familiar hadn't forgotten how dire our situation was. As I crouched down in the middle of our camp, seeing how much heat I could push into a flat stone I'd found without flames shooting up, the falcon swooped by, dropping a small bird and a rodent of some sort by my side. I gave him a salute he probably didn't notice, stuck the mushrooms and the eggs on the heated stone, and got to work plucking the feathers from the bird.

By the time the others stirred, I'd pulled together a halfway decent if very unusual spread for breakfast—or whatever this meal was exactly. I'd done it with a lot of help from the animals, but still. Cressida's nose twitched into a brief wrinkling at the smell of roasting rodent, which was cooking fur and all, but her eyes lit up eagerly a moment later as hunger kicked in. There wasn't much room for disgust when our options were this limited.

"You've been busy," she said to me in a softly chiding tone.

I shrugged and shot her the best grin I could summon in our present situation. "I couldn't sleep anymore. Figured I might as well see how mobile I can be."

I held back any mention of the possibility that I

wouldn't need to be all that mobile after all. She'd argue with me about me staying back—I knew that much. There was no point in hashing it out unless I was totally committed to the proposition.

Emeric shuffled off out of sight to relieve himself and returned with the same somber air he pretty much always seemed to have. To my chagrin, I couldn't help eyeing him surreptitiously as I finished my cooking.

I didn't swing that way, so I wasn't exactly the best judge of another man's attractiveness, but I could admit that he was definitely more built than I was, and probably kind of handsome in a solemn, square-jawed sort of way. And there was that titanium arm, which was admittedly pretty cool, even if the reasons for it were tragic.

He hadn't just convinced Cressida to follow him to Portland for his scheme. Somewhere along the way, he'd started putting moves on her. I couldn't blame her for keeping quiet about that with me—I was annoyed enough about it even now when I knew how pissed off she was with him. If I'd realized at the time...

I'd have kept things professional, of course. I wasn't a total washout of a baron-to-be. But it'd have made our chats a lot harder to bear, knowing she was falling for him every time she left to spend more time carrying out her schemes. Knowing it could have been me—it'd almost been me—if not for a few pointless rules and the pain I couldn't erase from her past.

He still wanted her. I didn't need magic to read the momentary softening of his eyes when his gaze lingered on her. Would he have made his promise if he hadn't been that invested? Would he have helped us escape at all?

Did it matter?

I shook off those thoughts and dished out our meal as fairly as I could across our sort-of plates. The eggs proved to be a little chewier than last time, but the mushrooms were still decent. The less said about the poor stringy bird and the rodent-of-some-kind, the better. All that mattered about the food was that I had a little less pain in my body once my stomach was partway full.

Emeric glanced around us with a couple of murmured casting words and then pointed off through the trees. "The town is that way. I don't know exactly how much farther. I don't really want to turn my phone on when I haven't gotten any reception in the woods so far—it's down to its last bit of battery, and we'll want that to call your barons once we get back to civilization."

Cressida nodded. Her gaze slid to me.

Before any of us could address the elephant in the room or, well, clearing—a.k.a., my mangled leg—Emeric's head snapped around. My pulse stuttered, my body tensing, but he didn't sound any alarm. Instead, he got slowly to his feet and peered through the trees in another direction.

"What?" Cressida asked, following his gaze.

"I could swear… But that doesn't make any sense." He took another couple of steps, and then he was loping out of sight through the trees.

I was about to shove myself up to see what was going on when he re-emerged, carrying a form about the size of a kitten in his arms. But it definitely wasn't shaped like a kitten. When it squirmed, turning its face toward us, I recognized it as a lizard. Its head was flat and wide with prickles protruding beneath its jaw, its long thin tail curling around Emeric's bicep.

"It's my familiar," Emeric said, shock plain in his voice. "I don't know how he could have gotten all the way out here—he should be home in his tank." He paused, and his face darkened.

Cressida sprang up. "The reapers must have gotten him. They knew he'd come to you."

"They haven't followed him, though. Nothing's triggered the wards." He glanced at me. "You haven't sensed anything threatening, have you?"

I shook my head, muttering a quick casting word to confirm it. "There could be magic *on* your familiar. They might have some reason they're delaying an attack."

Emeric murmured over the lizard, and his expression relaxed. "I'm not picking up anything. It's possible they meant to use him but he got away from them. Or they tried to follow him but he could tell they were up to no good and refused, so they threw him away." He frowned, rubbing the creature under its chin. "They probably figured he wouldn't make it. This isn't a good habitat for him. He's got to be freezing right now." He tucked the lizard deeper into his arms to warm it.

Cressida's brow creased with worry. "Here—we can cool down the stone Noah used for the cooking a little and maybe that could help warm him up."

Seeing her hustle Emeric over, testing her hand against

the stone that had already begun to cool, I had to reflect on how far *she* had come. I'd heard my brother and the other barons tell stories—wryly fond now that so much time had passed and so much had changed—about what a hard time Rory Bloodstone had when she'd first shown up at Blood U, and not just from her fellow scions. At some point, Cressida had helped a couple of her friends kidnap Rory's familiar. At another time, the three of them had egged one of their own animals on in trying to attack it.

Now, as angry and hurt as she was over Emeric's behavior, she was dropping everything to try to help his familiar. She still tensed up a bit when he leaned close to set the lizard down on the stone, but she managed a brief smile when Emeric thanked her.

She'd been allied with the reapers once, and now I trusted her to be on my side beyond any doubt. Who was to say that Emeric couldn't follow that same path? If she'd been able to make up for the sins of her past… we should probably give him a chance to too. He'd already made a pretty good start of it, hadn't he?

Even as I thought that, a different sense of resolve formed inside me. I swallowed my last bit of mushroom and stretched out my good leg, willing the stiffness out of the muscles.

I'd give him a chance, sure. But whether it was a stupid decision or not, no way in hell was I leaving Cressida to fend for herself alongside him if he changed his mind all over again.

CHAPTER THIRTEEN

Cressida

The dawning sun seeped through the trees, bringing color to the landscape that'd looked dull and gray in the dimness before. Seeing it at our left at least confirmed that we were heading in approximately the right direction.

We'd started taking turns casting numbing spells so Noah didn't buckle under the pain his leg was obviously causing him, and our slower pace while he lurched along had become increasingly apparent. To conserve our remaining magic, we'd decided not to expend the energy it took casting a spell across the remaining miles to confirm the town's location. Not unless we felt really turned around.

Noah clomped along beside me, still putting on an upbeat face, though his smile was stiffer than usual, his jaw clenched. He hadn't been talking much. Each step was clearly an effort: balance on his good leg, swing the stick-crutch ahead of him, brace himself against it, and hop to come level with it. I didn't think we'd been walking for more than a couple of hours, and the air still held some of the night's chill, but along his forehead, his hair had dampened with sweat.

We'd taken a break maybe an hour ago so he could catch his breath, although I'd claimed I needed one too. I'd debated whether we could construct some kind of stretcher out of branches that Emeric and I could carry him on, but even if Noah agreed—which was doubtful—I wasn't sure *my* ankle was up to that much stress.

Or the rest of me, for that matter. The queasiness that had lurked in my stomach yesterday had risen up sharper after our last meal. I was sweating too under my finally-dry dress, but not from the walk, which was pretty tame at Noah's pace. Periodic flushes of heat raced under my skin. I suspected I had a fever.

Just a light one. Not a big deal. Nothing at all to worry about as long as we made it across those last several miles to civilization without it getting significantly worse.

Emeric paused by a tree trunk. I was about to ask why when he plucked a beetle I hadn't noticed off the bark. He held it out to Lancer where the bearded dragon was still cradled under his other arm, but his familiar only eyed the insect and then let his head droop again.

It wasn't just the humans among us who were feeling unwell.

"He's still not warmed up enough?" I asked with a pang of sympathy. Percy had never gotten sick, but an eagle familiar had pounced on him once and damaged one of his wings to the point that he'd needed magical healing before he could fly again. It'd been unsettling enough having his pain ripple into me for that brief time.

Whatever else I could say when it came to Emeric, he clearly cared about his familiar.

"I don't know." Emeric tossed the bug away and stroked the lizard's head gently. "There's no way of telling how long he was out of his typical environment. Extended exposure could have a lasting effect. And he'll be stressed by being out here at all even if I've gotten him back to a good temperature."

"I don't think I've met anyone with a bearded dragon familiar before," Noah said a little breathlessly, pausing between lurching steps. "Interesting choice."

I didn't think he meant anything negative by that—he was just making conversation, maybe even trying to be a bit friendly after yesterday's blow-up where we'd almost sent Emeric off on his own—but Emeric's shoulders tensed. "So's a raccoon," he retorted.

Noah just grinned crookedly. "No argument there. He *has* come in handy for this adventure, though." He glanced through the trees to where he must have been able to sense Kato's presence and then back to Emeric. "I just meant people usually go with an animal that's a little more… mobile, or adaptable. Did you have a particular reason?"

As we started walking again, Emeric eyed the scion as if trying to read any ulterior motives through Noah's skull. Apparently he couldn't decipher any.

"I didn't expect to need to be all that mobile," he said. "We were living in the city, not some country estate where there was lots of room to roam—or where we didn't have to worry about someone calling animal control if they saw something odd on the loose. For my family, having a familiar was more like having a pet. My dad had an iguana, and I always liked playing around with her as a kid. She had a sense of humor." A faint smile touched his lips. "So I guess lizards are a family tradition."

The smile was bittersweet. He'd said his father had died two years ago in the battle between the old barons and the scions. I wondered what'd happened to his father's familiar, but the thought of poking at that wound more made my stomach twist. I kept my mouth shut.

Maybe it wasn't so surprising to imagine a guy who'd been through that, who'd lost that much, might have become warped by resentment enough to come up with a horrible plan. I hadn't exactly been an angel to most of my classmates during my first few years at Blood U. Sometimes the only way you could feel in control over your life was to exert whatever control you could over *whoever* you could.

"They've got medical staff at the university who are good with animals," I said. "They'll make sure he totally recovers."

Emeric shot me a startled look, as if it hadn't occurred to him *I'd* care what happened to his familiar. But I wasn't ready to offer more than that, even if I could relate to his past in some ways. I kept tramping along, pretending I hadn't noticed.

"It makes sense, wanting to follow a tradition like that," Noah said after a moment. "I probably didn't put enough value in the ones my family has. Ashgraves have been in the habit of picking hunting birds, so really I should have a familiar like Cressida's. But with so many other things kind of decided *for* me, I just had to strike out on my own path there."

He cocked his head at the forest around us and let his tone turn totally dry. "I'm starting to see breaking new ground isn't always the way to go."

A chuckle tumbled out of Emeric that appeared to surprise even him. After, he swiped his hand across his mouth, but I thought something had relaxed in his expression. "I'm with you there," he said in a low voice.

A few minutes later, Kato came trundling into view with something clamped against his chest with one of his front paws. Noah leaned down to take it from him and held up a dripping honeycomb, with only a few stray raccoon hairs and bits of dirt stuck to it. "Nice score," he told his familiar, picking those off. "I don't see any hawks or falcons come up with a treat like that." He winked at me before breaking off a small chunk and offered it. "*Pour mon papillon.*"

It really wasn't fair how his lilting accent could send a flutter of warmth through my chest—and lower—despite how wretched I felt otherwise. I decided it was better not to ask what he'd just called me and eyed the honeycomb. A couple of days ago, my mouth would have exploded with saliva at the sight, but today my stomach recoiled.

"No thanks," I said, and when concern darkened his

eyes, added quickly, "I just don't feel up to anything that sweet. I had plenty at breakfast."

Noah accepted my excuse, though the concern remained in his expression. He handed about half of the comb over to Emeric, who accepted it with much more enthusiasm than I'd been able to offer, including a "Thank you," that sounded remarkably genuine. Maybe he was starting to revise his opinion of scions—or at least this scion—just a little.

We'd just set off again, Noah showing impressive dexterity as he licked the remains of the honey off his fingers while leaning that arm on his crutch, when a rumbled growl carried through the trees.

All three of us froze, our heads swiveling toward the sound. My heart skipped a beat. A huge black bear was pushing through the underbrush toward us.

It heaved off the ground onto its hind legs, swaying slightly as it took in the three of us. Another growl reverberated from its maw.

My heart was outright racing now, but Emeric's brow had furrowed as if he was more confused than scared. "This doesn't make sense," he said. "From what my mom told me, black bears are usually more afraid of people than we are of them. She ran into a few in the country when she lived out there as a kid. They see you, they usually run off, not toward you."

"Maybe it got a whiff of that honey and thinks we stole a comb that belonged to it," I said quietly.

"Still…"

"It doesn't matter how strange this is," Noah broke in.

"It's here now, and it's definitely not running away. How do we make sure it *doesn't* charge at us? Did your mom tell you about that?"

Emeric wet his lips. If Noah's casual referral to the woman who'd abandoned his family irritated him, he kept it to himself. "I think… it was something about making yourself seem bigger and scarier than you really are. Wave your arms around, make lots of noise."

That sounded about as likely to enrage an already pissed off animal as to calm it down, but the amount *I* knew about dealing with bears was zilch. There might have been animals that big in the woods around the Warbury chalet, but my parents had kept wards up that discouraged all local wildlife as well as human intruders.

I raised my hands and swung my arms through the air like I was making a snow angel. "Hey, you, get out of here! We've got nothing for you!" I stomped my feet for good measure. Emeric waved and hollered too, and Noah shook his crutch.

The bear made a fierce groaning sound and stepped closer to us.

I swallowed hard. "Um, I don't think that's working." Every nerve in my body was screaming at me to get away, but I doubted I could outrun that thing—and Noah definitely couldn't. I wasn't leaving him.

I fumbled for a spell to push it back, not sure whether I had the energy but willing to try my best if I had no other choice. As I eased forward to put myself between the bear and Noah, he made a noise of protest.

But Emeric was moving forward too. He intoned a few

casting words that vibrated with magical power. Nothing that was propelling the bear back, because its massive form didn't budge. But its paws came down, its head bobbing as it studied him. It didn't growl again. I guessed that was a minor win.

"That's right," Emeric said, his voice strained. How much energy were those castings taking out of him? "Go on back to whatever you were doing. There's nothing interesting to see here. No one's trying to hurt you. Everything's fine." He murmured another few syllables and then another.

The bear shuffled backward and lowered onto four legs. It let out a huff that sounded mildly annoyed. Noah and I stayed perfectly still and silent.

Finally, the creature heaved around and lumbered off through the trees in the direction it'd come. Emeric's shoulders sagged as he exhaled raggedly.

Noah peered past me at him. "What kind of spell was that?"

"I was aiming for a soothing effect. Hard to know what a bear will find soothing, though." Emeric shook his head. "I was a little worried I'd just piss it off more."

"Obviously not." I arched my eyebrows at him, a little of my sense of humor returning in the wake of the adrenaline surge. "If you can talk a bear into chilling out that easily, imagine what you could do for people. Ever consider a career in therapy?"

The muscle in Emeric's jaw twitched. I winced inwardly, sensing I'd hit a sore spot before he even spoke. "I think I've done enough of that on my own time. I got some practice helping my sister get through the first few months after Dad died."

Because he'd been the only one she had. Who could Emeric have turned to with his own grief? The assholes he'd been trying to impress back in Portland obviously hadn't given a shit about him or his feelings.

He turned away, his posture stiffening again as if he wished he hadn't mentioned that. As if he thought *we* might use the information against him.

"I'm sorry," I said quickly. "I didn't mean—"

"I know." He didn't sound upset, only resigned. "We'd better get going. I don't know what was wrong with that bear, but I'd rather not find out if there are more like that wandering around here."

"No argument there," Noah said easily enough, and I wished as I had a gazillion times before that I had more of the casual warmth that came so easily to him.

The sun was getting higher, burning off what'd remained of the cool night. As we trudged onward, its heat wrapped around me. My stomach churned harder. Good thing I hadn't eaten that honey. I wasn't sure I could keep anything down right now.

Maybe I'd feel better once we had a chance to rest again. Soon we'd have to for Noah's sake anyway. Just keep going a little longer, one foot after the other. One foot—

I stalled as the ground beneath my toes crumbled away. The guys stopped on either side of me. We stared at the latest hurdle the forest had thrown at us: a narrow, steep-sided gulley at least twenty feet deep and several feet across.

CHAPTER FOURTEEN

Cressida

Staring at the chasm in the forest floor, Noah let out a dull laugh. "Well, I don't think any of us are jumping that."

Yeah, no. *Maybe* if I'd flung myself hard enough, I could have reached the nearly sheer slope on the other side, but the tangle of vegetation along its edge didn't look stable enough to offer a definite hold. Chances were I'd either plummet the equivalent of two stories into the bottom of the little gulley or break a few limbs against that slope before sliding down.

And Noah definitely wasn't leaping any distance in his current condition.

Emeric frowned, tucking his familiar close against his side and toeing the edge on our side of the chasm. The earth crumbled, still damp and sticky from yesterday's downpour. Some of it clung to his shoes.

He shook the mud off and peered along the length of the chasm. "It'll have to get narrower and shallower at some point, or else there could be a fallen tree across it. And of course the road must go over it—we could cross there."

And put ourselves back in the reapers' sights with Noah in no condition to make a run for it any more than he could jump. Out of the three of us, the soon-to-be baron was the one they wanted the most. My stomach knotted, the tension bringing out a deeper swell of nausea. "I say we head away from the road. The reapers might even have realized we'll have to navigate around this gully and be paying special attention to that stretch of road."

Noah nodded, accepting my decision without complaint even though he was the one it affected most either way. I suspected if I'd said we should try the bridge, he'd have accepted that too. Didn't he know it mattered just as much to me to see him safely out of here as to escape our enemies myself?

And it really did. That surge of protective emotion overwhelmed the tension and the queasiness inside me. For a second, all my awareness narrowed in on his handsome, stoically optimistic face. He was the one with the gouged-up leg, but I wasn't sure *I'd* have made it this far without him by my side.

Even if I'd have let myself act on those feelings, now wouldn't have been the time for it. We set off along the edge of the chasm, eyeing the drop beneath us and the distance to the opposite bank carefully.

After enough tramping to send sweat trickling down

my back, the gully wasn't looking any more traversable than before. I sucked my lower lip under my teeth, unable to stop myself from nibbling at it, and eyed the forest around me. "Maybe we should just create our own bridge? Magically chop down a tree?"

Emeric's brow furrowed. "I could try… It'd take a fair bit of energy just splitting the wood, though. Where I'm at, even if I scare up a little more power from the wildlife, I don't think I could stop it from crashing over."

And that loud a sound might alert the reapers if they were anywhere nearby.

"If we all pitch in, we should be able to at least partly control the fall," Noah said.

I wavered, but I didn't like the idea of wandering much farther off track any more than that of the reapers descending on us. "Let's see what creatures we can terrify while we keep walking, and if we haven't found a better way by the time we're juiced up, we'll give it a shot then."

There didn't seem to be a whole lot of wildlife around here, though. Percy startled a few songbirds flitting between the trees a short distance away, but I didn't catch many flickers of fear passing into me directly from the terrain around us. From Emeric's deepening frown, I guessed he wasn't either. He stroked Lancer's back, the lizard not in any shape to pitch in.

Well, maybe we'd end up walking far enough that our problem solved itself, then. I picked up my pace to catch up with Noah, who'd managed to pull ahead of me even with his lurching gait, and at the same moment he set his crutch down on the wrong patch of soil near the edge of the gully.

The dirt broke off in a clod beneath his weight and tumbled into the chasm, the crutch dropping with it. Noah stumbled after it. He snatched at a nearby tree, but only broke off a twig as he plummeted over the edge.

My heart stuttering, I threw myself after him. I caught his arm, but I landed right at the crumbly, muddy edge, and my body slipped over the side too. With a thump and a tug of my shirt, I realized Emeric had made a similar miscalculation.

The steep slope was even muddier farther down where no sunlight had reached it to dry out the soil. Even as I scrambled for something to catch hold of, we slid faster. Emeric spat out a few casting words, and the earth gripped us—not enough to stop our fall, but slowing it down.

Thanks to him, we hit the narrow floor of the gully with a bump instead of a crash. Noah still hissed through his teeth at the impact on his leg. He closed his eyes, his face going pale as he rode out the pain.

I heaved myself upright and spun around, taking in our new situation. My spirits sank so low they might as well have burrowed into the ground beneath my feet.

The gully bottom offered us about three feet in width of muddy, rocky soil, framed by two all-but-sheer sides. I tried to grip one of the rocks embedded in the dirt, and it just pulled right out of the earth.

Percy glided by far above us with a whiff of concern. Too bad he wasn't anywhere near big enough to haul us out.

"Great," Emeric muttered. He glanced down at Lancer, who he'd managed to shield from any damage during our slide, and then eyed the edge of the slope above us—the edge we'd wanted to reach. Squaring his shoulders, he held out his other hand—the titanium one —and spoke a casting word at the mottled dirt in front of us.

The soil hardened into a solid strip about a foot wide from the base of the gully to knee height. With another word, Emeric shaped a foothold into it. Then, with a strain entering his voice, he drew his earthen ladder a little taller, until it reached the level of my waist. He added another notch for climbing there.

His next breath came with a rasp. I looked at him more closely—almost all of the color had seeped from his face too. My pulse skipped for a totally different reason. "Emeric, if you're too drained—"

"I have to keep going," he said, his voice wrenchingly ragged. "I swore to get you two out of these woods safe no matter what I had to do. If I don't—"

His titanium arm twitched as if the muscles that guided it were trying to tug it toward his head. He quickly grated out another casting word, raising the path of solid dirt another couple of feet.

A wave of cold washed over me. His oath was activating. If he didn't keep up his casting—and it would take dozens more spells to extend that makeshift ladder to the top of the chasm—he'd find himself shattering his skull.

I'd have protested that it shouldn't count if his stores

were depleted, but it obviously did anyway. A mage was never truly without recourse. If you didn't have any outside energy stored up, your own fear could fuel you—while eating away at you bit by bit until you weren't much more than a hollow husk.

Even if Emeric managed to avoid bashing his brains in, he might not have much of a life left by the time he completed his commitment to the oath anyway.

I stepped closer, my lungs constricting. "Let me help. I can do some of it. How are you shaping the dirt?" I'd never had to condense soil into a solid surface to hold a person's weight before—I wasn't sure how I'd go about it.

Emeric shook his head, which was already drooping. "I don't think I can stop to try to explain it," he said hoarsely. "I'm not sure it'd even work if you—if you knew. I'm supposed to take care of you two *myself*."

He sputtered the casting word again on the heels of that statement, only managing to extend the solid strip about the height of his hand. It was as tall as me now, but that was less than a third of the total distance.

I whipped around, searching for something, anything that could at least make his job easier. The last thing I expected was for Noah to jerk to his feet.

The scion had managed to hold onto his crutch all the way down. He planted it against the gully's floor with a meaningful thump, his mouth still tight with pain but his eyes brightly alert, and spoke in a steady, determined tone I'd never heard from him before.

"Emeric, we're going to get you some more magic so you can do this without hurting yourself. It isn't a violation of your oath. You need the energy first so that you can help us properly. All right?"

He sounded almost like Declan—like Declan in his role as Baron Ashgrave, laying down the law. Emeric shot him a startled look, but the muscles at the upper end of his titanium arm relaxed a little. Noah's framing must have sunk in in a way that the oath would accept. "All right. How do we do that?"

Yeah. There weren't any creatures down here to frighten—earthworms and millipedes didn't give enough of a shit what we did to offer anything like real terror to fuel us.

Noah motioned with his free hand toward me and then the top of the gully. "Take a few of those scraps of energy you've been using on the dirt and add them to Cressida's magic as she conjures an illusion. Maybe a bear inspired by our recent friend? Something that can rampage through the woods without making too much noise but threatening enough to send every prey animal for a mile around into a panic. Since you've helped her, you'll get a portion of the benefit."

He turned toward me, his gaze finding mine with the same air of unshakeable certainty he'd summoned from somewhere inside him. Maybe he *was* channeling Declan the same way he wanted me to draw on our clash with the bear.

But it didn't really matter where it was coming from. If I'd ever wondered what Noah as a baron would be like to experience, I was getting him now. He still had the same warmth, but it was laid over a sense of authority all my instincts immediately wanted to bow to.

"Are you up to that?" he asked. Not whether I'd do it, only if I was capable of it. Because if I was, he was all but ordering me as one of my rulers to cast the illusion he'd asked for. Something about his tone and the imperious look on his face sent a tingle right down the center of me.

Of course, he didn't need to order me. It was a reasonable plan, one I wished I'd thought of, and I'd rather dredge up my last shreds of energy to put them toward this than watch Emeric kill himself trying to fulfill his promise.

"No problem," I said with a tip of my head, already picturing the fiercest creature I could depict to strike fear into as many animal hearts as possible.

If only I could have terrorized some of the reapers who'd set us off on the course to begin with. Well, maybe I'd get a chance to pay them back later.

With my monstrous bear in mind, I turned to Emeric. "Ready?"

He nodded. Sensing my need, Percy found a cluster of sparrows to dive-bomb, providing me with a fresh burst of energy.

I let a casting word slip off my tongue, picturing the form I was willing into sight and sound on the terrain above, and Emeric lifted his roughened voice to join mine.

A quiver of his energy, shaky and fraught as he tore it from himself, melded with mine. Then a faint bellow echoed overhead where my illusion had come into being. With another word and a flick of my fingers, I sent it barging through the brush, swinging its massive claws this way and that.

Since I couldn't see the woods it was moving through, it'd end up passing straight through branches and bushes. That was fine. I didn't think the animals would notice when I'd added the fierce roar and the feral scent I'd caught a whiff of from the real bear to my construction. They weren't going to stick around and give it a full logistical analysis.

And yes, a stream of fear was already shuddering into my chest, jolts from all different scampering bodies above twining together into a mix that soothed my nerves as it reached me. It wasn't going to be anywhere near as much as I usually had stored up when I was at school and not in the middle of a desperate bid for survival, but it was more than I'd had in days.

A faint bloom of color was coming back into Emeric's face. He shot me a smile so openly relieved and thankful, softening the grim lines of his face, and damn it if my pulse didn't hiccup in a much more enjoyable way.

But the shift of Noah's posture brought my gaze back to him immediately. He was watching me, his own face lit up with admiration—and a little pride, I thought, that he'd pulled us together the way he had. In that moment, my heart overflowed with another rush of emotion, one I had to put a name to now.

I loved this guy—this not-quite-baron who could bring a laugh into the direst of situations but put his foot down when he needed to, who had an Ashgrave's iron will beneath all that easygoing charm. And for the first time since my attraction to him had first sparked into being within my ribcage, I didn't recoil from the sensation.

I'd always known he had the spirit of a baron in him, hadn't I? Watching him take charge had unearthed a shiver of sensation from all the way back when I'd woken up next to him in my dorm-room bed. It hadn't been just the university administration's view on breaking the rules I'd been afraid of, or what my overstep meant about me. No, some part of me had been scared of how *he'd* feel in his position of authority. Of how quickly he could crush the little happiness I'd found at Blood U if he ever regretted what he'd done.

He wouldn't have hurt me. I wasn't worried about that now that I knew him better. But... I hadn't ever really been at risk of hurting *him* either. It really wasn't at all like what had happened between Shane Harrowfell and me. I hadn't wanted to think about the power Noah technically held over me, but it'd been there all along—a hell of a lot more than I'd had over him as his TA.

I hadn't exploited him or abused his trust. Out of what couldn't be called anything worse than a certain amount of selfishness, I'd broken a rule that hadn't been much more than a formality given our respective positions. I'd forgiven myself for so many things more awful than that already.

So why couldn't I let that one mistake go when the only theoretical victim of it seemed to want to absolve me of it even more than I did?

I didn't have the answer to that question firmly in my grasp, but it felt a lot closer than it ever had before. As I smiled back at Noah, a strange lightness came over me.

But before any of us could act on any unexpected revelations, we needed to get out of this damned gully.

Emeric had gotten back to work solidifying the path of earth with its footholds up the slope. I moved in to join him, not risking my inexperience with physicality on the main work, but scooping out a few additional handholds for easier climbing.

"What about Noah?" I had to ask. He wasn't going to be able to clamber up when he could barely use his one leg.

Emeric had just built our ladder of sorts to the top of the chasm. He turned to study the other guy. In a steadier voice than before, he summoned a larger mass of dirt into a cushion-sized lump that jutted solidly from the slope.

"Sit there," he told the scion, and glanced at me. "Your illusion petered out. Can we conjure another one to make sure I'll have enough power?"

I nodded, and we cast together, me propelling the image of the rampaging bear onto the opposite side of the gully this time. As more flashes of fear trickled into me as they must have Emeric, he fixed his gaze on the seat he'd fashioned and pushed it up the slope with the force of his voice and a sweep of his arms.

It took a few minutes and a beading of sweat over Emeric's skin. Noah teetered once, holding his crutch tight. As soon as he could reach the vegetation along the edge, he hauled himself out, dragging his bad leg. "Impressive teamwork," he called down. "Now get yourselves out of here, and I'll see if I can't contribute more next time."

Did he not even realize that we might never have pulled this off at all without him? "You did plenty," I insisted, grasping the handholds when Emeric gestured for me to go first. "Benefits of having a scion along."

He gave a disbelieving laugh, and I resolved that by the time we made it out of this mess, he wouldn't doubt those words.

Assuming we did ever make it out. Lord only knew what we'd have to face next.

CHAPTER FIFTEEN

Cressida

I woke to the softly fading light of evening. Crickets were chirping in the depths of the forest. The summer heat was ebbing, but thankfully the air was nowhere near as cool as it'd gotten right after the thunderstorm.

I closed my eyes again, but my thoughts darted around in my head too restlessly for me to imagine I was getting back to sleep. After tackling the chasm, none of us had felt up to much more of a hike. We'd trudged along for about another hour before calling it quits at the first stream we'd encountered. We'd collapsed into a rough camp here, only pausing long enough to have a quick wash and cast our usual protective wards.

I couldn't say it'd been the most restful doze I'd ever had, but I figured I'd been asleep a good five or six hours all told. That was pretty good these days. I was so worn out that even the hard ground and poor excuse for a bed couldn't stop me from zonking out.

Smothering a yawn, I sat up, careful to avoid the sunshade I'd hastily built to cover my face from the daylight. Emeric was still sleeping, his head resting on his titanium arm while he kept the one of flesh curled around Lancer, who shivered where he was nestled against his master's chest. The former reaper looked younger in sleep—less grim and more relaxed. I could almost picture him a few years back when he'd have been finishing his studies at Blood U.

What would his life have been like if he hadn't gotten caught up in the conflict between the old barons and their scions—if there'd been no conflict at all? If he'd kept his arm and his father… Of course, none of the rest of this would have happened in that case, and I'd probably never have met him. But I found myself wishing he could have had a chance at that future without so much pain and resentment weighing him down.

None of us had been given easy choices back then, had we?

I pulled my eyes away. Noah's rumpled mat of leaves lay empty, but he hadn't gone far yet. My ears caught the faint thump of his crutch—it sounded like he was heading toward the stream.

I hesitated, not sure he'd even want company, but ever since the moment of revelation I'd had watching the baron in him, I'd been wanting to talk to him. I'd put him through enough stress already with my unintentional hot-

and-cold routine without dragging out his uncertainty about my feelings even longer.

If I could have been sure we'd survive the next couple of days and reach the safety I assumed lay beyond the woods, I might have waited until we were secure and comfortable back at Blood U to say anything. But I didn't have that certainty… and if the reapers caught us, if they disposed of me the way they probably intended to at this point, I didn't want to die with Noah thinking I still believed that accepting *his* feelings would be a mistake.

I eased onto my feet gingerly so as not to disturb Emeric and crept between the trees in the direction of the lurching steps. They stopped a few moments later when Noah must have reached the stream. As I left the campsite behind, I picked up my pace a little, wanting to make sure I caught him before he headed back. I might not be feeling quite as hostile toward Emeric right now, but this wasn't the kind of conversation I'd like spectators for.

The trees thinned along the bank of the burbling stream, one of the largest we'd encountered on our trek. From wading into it for a quick splash all over earlier, I knew the water was deep enough in the middle to come up to my thighs.

Noah looked up at my arrival. He'd hunkered down at the edge of the stream, his back propped against a tree and his bad leg stretched out in front of him, the other drawn up at a casual angle. He pulled the water bottle he'd been filling out of the stream and offered me a smile that was weary enough to send a pang through my chest.

"How're you doing?" he asked, as if he had anywhere

near as many reasons to worry about my well-being as I did about his.

I sat down a short distance from him and shucked off my sneakers so I could dip my newly calloused feet into the cool water. The light chill brought out the stinging of my battered soles briefly before soothing it. The sleep had left my head less muggy than it'd been for most of the past day, and my stomach only pinched with hunger. The nausea might come back when I tried to eat, but I'd take the reprieve for now.

"Not too bad," I said, and tilted my head toward his leg. "You? Do you want me to help with another numbing spell?"

His mouth slanted into a wry grimace. "Nah, I just cast one myself. I should look for some more moss and see what Emeric can make of it if he'll change the dressing. But there's probably nothing much to do for it until we can get to proper professionals. I'm sure I'll manage until then."

Of course he would. Noah's determined optimism wouldn't allow for anything else. I splashed my feet gently in the current, debating how to bring up the subject I'd meant to talk about. It seemed too awkward to just blurt out, *By the way, I've decided you're really too wonderful to keep resisting, so do you want to actually date or something?*

I ran my tongue over my lips, resting my hands against the soft tufts of grass sprouting from the forest floor. "You were pretty impressive this morning, you know. Talking Emeric through the whole oath thing, getting us on track. You're going to make a fantastic baron."

Noah sputtered a laugh that was much more disbelieving than I'd have expected. "You think so? I've got high standards to live up to. After all his preparation and dedication, Declan already fills the Baron Ashgrave role about ten times over."

My gaze snapped to him, and he gave me a crooked smile, but I could tell from the hint of sadness in it that he wasn't just joking around. "Has he said he doesn't think you should be co-baron with him when you're finished with school?"

Noah's gaze slid away from me toward the trees. "Oh, no, nothing like that. He was nervous about me taking on the responsibility, but mostly because of the target it paints on my back."

He picked up a pebble and flicked it into the stream, managing to make it skip so it ricocheted onto the opposite bank. "That's kind of the problem right there, though, isn't it? He's spent so much time protecting me, I never really had to prepare to be a baron. Kind of hard to catch up when you're more than a decade behind. Not that I blame him. He had no idea we'd end up sharing the position. And it's not like I ever pushed back all that hard against *being* protected. I had my fun off in Paris…"

He trailed off, but I could fill in the blank. He'd had his fun, and meanwhile Declan had been fending off attacks from all sides back at Blood U. From their aunt, from the older barons who'd seen Declan as the weakest link and an impediment to their plans. He'd definitely shielded Noah from a lot.

Noah was smart enough to realize why I'd be worried about leaving things unspoken. He didn't dwell on that part of what I'd said, though. He just smiled, cupping my face so he could angle it to meet my eyes. "If that's the only good thing that comes out of this trek, then I'll still call it a win."

I laughed, and then we were kissing again, more ravenously than before. God, I could have been having this bliss for weeks if I hadn't been so caught up in past traumas and doubts. Suddenly all that mattered was getting as much out of *this* moment as I could.

Because who knew if we'd get another one.

Noah tugged me closer, and I melded against him, lips to lips, chest to chest, as if we could become one being. His kisses captured my mouth with all the same desperate passion ringing through me. His hand skimmed up and down my side in a teasing stroke that summoned more torturous anticipation with every repetition.

Finally, he molded it to the curve of my breast, as careful as if we'd never done this before. In a way, it was like it *was* our first time—a new first time. Our first time sober, our first time really understanding each other.

I pressed into his touch with an encouraging noise in my throat that turned into a gasp when he swept his thumb over my nipple. The heat coursing through me flared, searing low in my belly.

Noah let out a sound that was almost a growl. "There's so much I want to do to you. *With* you," he murmured, his voice husky with desire and a thread of regret. I could only imagine how this might have gone without his leg holding him back.

But the same desire was burning through me, and there were *some* things we could do. To confirm our connection. To dismiss all the missteps and pains from before.

Careful of his wounded leg, I slipped my knee over his lap to straddle him. Noah gripped my waist, gazing up at me with so much hunger I nearly caught fire in the moment before he pulled my lips back to his. My hips moved of their own accord, grinding the spot where I was neediest against the bulge in his jeans.

Noah groaned. He adjusted his position against the tree so he could lift up to meet me just slightly without provoking his injury. With each rock of our bodies pressing together, more pleasure rushed up from between my legs. My breaths grew shaky, my kisses rougher.

Noah squeezed my breast and guided me with his other hand on my hip. Soft words in French spilled from his mouth between kisses. "*Je suis fou de toi. Mon ange.*" I had no idea what he was saying, but maybe he had an inkling just how much the simple sound of the words turned me on. I whimpered, kissing him harder.

He might have been thinking I'd be satisfied with getting off just like this, grinding against each other. But right then, I didn't give a damn about the darkening forest around us or whatever birds or beasts might witness this intimate act. I just wanted him, as much of him as I could have. I wanted to *give* him all I could of me.

My sex clenched with a fresh wave of arousal, and I

forced myself to resist the careening momentum we'd already built up. I pushed myself to my feet to wrench off my panties. Noah watched, his eyes darkening.

I'd intended to sink right back down, but before I could, he caught my thighs and drew me closer. "*Venez á moi, ma chérie.*" A heady tingling shot through me just at the words. Then he slid the skirt of my dress up, in the perfect position to bring his mouth to my core.

Oh. I hadn't meant—hadn't expected— I was hit by a momentary flash of embarrassment, as well as relief that I'd washed down there as well as I could when we'd stopped for the day. But when the heat of Noah's mouth closed over my clit, the burst of pleasure washed every other sensation away.

Another whimper worked its way from my throat. I grasped the smooth stands of his hair, clinging on, swaying with the movements of his lips. He devoured me, teasing so much bliss from my sensitive folds with the slick of his tongue that my legs started to wobble.

I tipped forward to rest my forehead against the trunk of the tree before I toppled right over. "Oh, God."

He hummed in approval from deep in his chest, the sound reverberating into me in a way that only heightened the pleasure. I swallowed my moans as well as I could, biting my lip as he plundered me even more thoroughly. The heady sensation swelled and swelled, his hands clutching me tight, his mouth scorching me, until ecstasy exploded inside me in a wave that lit stars behind my eyes.

I let my legs buckle, dropping over him and reaching for the fly of his jeans as soon as it was in reach. Noah's breath came ragged as he helped me hitch his pants far enough down over his hips to free his erection. When I curled my fingers around the silky solid length, another groan escaped him.

He grazed his fingers along my slit. "Let me?"

I understood without any clarification. At my nod, he rasped out the spell that spread a faint tingling inside me—protecting me from the consequences that would only matter if we survived this trip anyway. But that was Noah, looking out for me, trying to do what was best for me.

I just hoped I could be as good to him as he'd been to me already.

The moment he'd completed the casting, I lined myself up over him and plunged down. Our mouths crashed together at the same time, my musky flavor on his lips, but all I cared about was the wonderful feeling of being stretched and filled, of encompassing this man that *I* had chosen in every possible way.

Noah couldn't arch very far to meet me, but he was far from a passive participant. He gripped my thighs, adjusting my angle against him, thrusting into me even deeper. Another climax built inside me, spiking through my nerves like a sizzling wick on a string of dynamite. I bucked against him, chasing that release, urging him toward his own.

Noah's fingers dug into my skin, just hard enough to amplify the spiral of pleasure. With a choked sound, I clenched around him. His muscles went rigid beneath me as he followed me over the edge.

As the high of the orgasm rippled through me and

faded away, we stayed there, interlocked in our embrace. Noah stroked his hand over my hair, seeking out my mouth for another kiss. The tenderness of that last brush of his mouth against mine brought out a surge of affection in my chest so powerful it propelled the words right off my tongue.

"I love you," I said, soft but clear. I hadn't been sure I was going to admit that much just yet, and the moment the declaration tumbled out, my chest constricted with a panic I couldn't explain. But only for the instant before Noah gathered me in his arms so tightly you'd have thought he never meant to let me go.

"I love you too," he said, sounding choked. "So much. I know you have trouble seeing it, Cressida, but you're fucking amazing."

I swallowed hard and dipped my head to nestle it against his shoulder. Who was I to argue with him after what we'd shared?

I just had to hope I was amazing enough to see us through whatever horrors we'd face next.

CHAPTER SIXTEEN

Cressida

My braid was sticking to the back of my neck, so damp with sweat it left a wet trail when I tugged it to the side. Today's sun had burned away any lingering relief from the thunderstorm. The forest felt like a furnace. I found myself missing the rain, as uncomfortable as it'd been at the time.

Unfortunately, the heat had brought back my nausea in full force, along with periodic waves of dizziness. After walking for a few hours last night, we'd stopped partway for another rest and then to gather food, but by the time the sun had risen, I hadn't been able to stomach the thought of eating. I'd lied and said I'd already eaten my share of the berries Kato had led me to and only nibbled at the one small bird I'd taken from Percy's hunt.

Noah might have suspected I was suffering more than I was letting on—not that he was in any position to talk with his stoicism over his leg. I glanced over at him and caught him watching me with an unusually serious expression. But as soon as our eyes met, his solemnness broke with one of those brilliant smiles that never failed to make my heart flutter.

Only now it wasn't a futile sensation. I'd owned my feelings, and he returned them—and I could keep at this for him without complaining, as long as it took for us to get home. An answering smile crossed my lips in return.

We *had* to make it home. No way was I giving up the most incredible connection I'd ever shared with anyone before I'd had much of a chance to even enjoy it.

It couldn't be far to the town now. When we'd risked reaching out with magic this morning to confirm we were still on the right track, the pulse of electric energy that emanated from Jondale had felt so much closer than the last time. I kept daydreaming that I spotted a telephone pole or a streetlamp up ahead through the trees.

Or maybe sunstroke was giving me hallucinations now too.

I rubbed my forehead, trying not to dwell on the unsteadiness of my thoughts or the growing grittiness in the back of my mouth. Not only was it hot, but we hadn't come across another stream since the one we'd left behind yesterday evening after my brief interlude with Noah. We'd drained the last of the water in the bottles overnight. I was tempted to lick my arm just to steal back the droplets of steam forming there.

Emeric coughed in a short, rough burst. Maybe he wasn't feeling so great either. None of us wanted to complain when we knew we were all pretty miserable as it was.

The former reaper's voice came out with a rasp that told me he was just as parched as I was. "I'll try another water seeking spell. Maybe there's something closer now."

I nodded. He'd attempted one when we'd first set out, but there hadn't been any stream close enough for him to locate, at least not one large enough that he'd picked up on its presence at a distance. A town made a whole lot more of an impression on the environment than some little brook.

Emeric murmured a casting word, his head swiveling to take in the landscape as we tramped on. Noah didn't speak, his breath hitching a bit with each heaved hop following the swing of his crutch. We were going to have to take another break soon for his sake if not all of ours, as much as I wanted to run all the way to Jondale right now.

To be fair, in my present state I wasn't sure I'd have made it there much faster anyway. Our current pace was about as much as my weakening legs could handle. And the closer we got to civilization, the closer our pursuers were likely to be lurking. We couldn't risk leaving Noah on his own with only his dwindled stores of magic to protect himself, especially not when he'd be their primary target.

The fact that he hadn't even suggested the idea in his noble way implied that even he didn't think it'd be wise.

We'd trudged along several steps farther when Emeric jerked to a halt. He pointed to our right—in the direction of the road, but we'd veered so far away from it before that I wasn't sure it mattered. "Over there. I caught just a tiny sense… I don't think it's a ton of water, but I'll take what I can get at this point."

"Detour!" Noah announced, somehow managing to sound jovial as well as weary.

Emeric led the way, setting off on an angle so that we were still moving generally toward the town at the same time. Lancer, who was crouched on his shoulder now that the weather had warmed, sank lower, tucking his scaled head against Emeric's neck.

The bearded dragon might have been happier with the current temperature, but he still looked pretty droopy. The only living being in our party who hadn't seemed at all bothered by the long trek was Kato, who I guessed was in his element. Percy was longing for a good soar in the open sky.

After maybe twenty minutes, the faint gurgle of running water reached my ears. My throat panged, and I managed to push myself a little faster.

The stream—well, it was so narrow and shallow that maybe "creek" was a better word—turned out to lie at the bottom of a shallow basin a short trek down a low but uneven slope. Noah paused at the top of the ridge, peering through the brush below.

"Wait here," I told him before he could attempt the descent. Even if he made it down the slope no problem, it'd take a lot out of him hauling himself back up it. "I'll fill your bottle first."

Noah's mouth twitched as if he'd held back a grimace, but he must have recognized the same things I had. He nodded and sank down on a bit of clear dirt to rest his legs.

Emeric had already nestled Lancer in a patch of sun hitting the base of a tree and headed down to the creek, pulling the bottles out of his pack as he went. I hurried after him, swaying a little as the sweltering breeze washed over me. When I reached the edge of the creek, I dropped to my knees, not caring that the mud there immediately stuck to my skin.

I grabbed one of the bottles, but I couldn't hold myself back from scooping a little water into my mouth first. It looked clear enough in my hand, but the taste was faintly earthly with an aftertaste of algae. Lovely. After this trip, I was going to treasure every gulp of tap water I got, that was for sure.

The cool liquid still soothed my throat, even if it made my stomach churn a little harder. I swallowed just enough to ward off my dizziness and then dunked the bottle I planned to bring back to Noah into the thin current, holding it as high off the silty bottom as I could while getting water in the opening.

When it was full to the brim, I hustled up to Noah's position, handed it to him, and headed back down to see about more hydration for myself. It was only a second before I heard him tipping it back to drink. Something in my gut relaxed despite my queasiness.

We'd be okay for a little longer. *He'd* be okay.

A short rest in general couldn't hurt him. I took a little more time filling my own water bottle. When I'd drained about half of it and refilled it again, I crouched lower to splash some water on my face as well.

Emeric had already gotten the same idea. His tawny hair stood up in damp spikes where he'd run his wet fingers through it. I glanced back toward Noah, glad I could make out his lean figure through the brush to confirm nothing was threatening him here, and Emeric's gaze followed mine.

"He matters a lot to you," he said.

I stiffened automatically, even though there hadn't been any accusation in his voice. "He's the best person I know," I said. "And he's always been there for me... even when I didn't realize it."

I hadn't even been thinking about the people who hadn't had my back, but Emeric clearly picked up on that implication anyway. He ducked his head, swiping his hand across his mouth.

My stomach twisted with something other than queasiness. We were dealing with enough problems without even more tensions stirred up between us. And I wasn't sure I was all that angry with Emeric anymore besides. He'd made some very shitty choices, but he'd gone farther than I'd ever have imagined to make up for them. Maybe it was starting to balance out.

"I didn't mean—" I started.

"No. It's okay. Even if you had meant it, I'd deserve it." Emeric let out a breath and looked down at his hands. His knuckles had paled where he was gripping his water bottle. "I know how badly I screwed up. I know whatever could have happened between us, I threw it away. I was only mentioning it because—whatever the two of *you* have, you don't need to hide it from me. I'm not going to throw a fit over it or something. You shouldn't have to force yourself to keep your distance from each other because of me."

A flush crept over my cheeks. Had he seen or heard something yesterday evening, or had he just picked up on a shift in the atmosphere between me and Noah? I *had* been careful not to act overly affectionate with the other guy, despite the occasional urges that'd struck me to grasp his hand or pull him into a kiss. But maybe our deepening connection had been obvious anyway.

I picked up a twig and idly prodded the damp dirt with it. "Oh. That—that's good to know." It was actually kind of gallant for Emeric to bother saying it. He could have left us awkwardly uncertain of how much we could reveal without setting off some new conflict.

Suddenly it felt important for me to clarify something too. "Just in case you wondered, I wasn't... *with* him while we were in Portland. I thought I couldn't be. Not that I saw you as just a rebound or something. I was interested in you for you—or who I thought you were—" I made a face at my stumbling words. "Anyway, my point is that while my family might not have given me the best ever grounding in caring relationships, as you've probably gathered, I wasn't just using you or cheating on anyone or —or anything. I wouldn't want to."

Emeric raised his eyes then. His gaze was so intense it sent a more potent flare of heat over my skin. "I didn't think you would." He swallowed audibly. "Everything—all the times we spent together in Portland—they weren't really a sham on my side either. I had an idea in my head that I could take some kind of revenge on you by getting you invested and then pushing you away, but *I* just kept getting more and more invested no matter how much I tried to block out those feelings…"

My throat constricted. "You don't have to explain."

"I do," he said. "To be clear, I'm not asking for anything now. I just— You're so much more than I gave you credit for, and I wish I'd seen it soon enough to stop us from ending up in this awful situation. As it is, I'll be happy if we come out of this with our lives and you at least not seeing me as the enemy. That'll be enough."

He got up without giving me a chance to respond and headed back up the slope toward Noah. I lingered for a moment longer, willing my emotions to settle into some kind of order, not sure what to make of his declaration.

I didn't know what to do about it, but I did believe him. He'd sounded more honest than I'd ever heard him, as raw as when he'd sworn that oath.

It shouldn't have mattered to me, but somehow it did anyway.

I dragged in a breath and headed after him. Now that we'd had a quick break, we should try to cover more distance before we stopped for a longer rest.

Noah had put the lid back on his bottle, which was only half full now. I held my hand out to take it from him. "Let me top that up, and then we can get going."

He shot me a soft little smile that lit me up inside. But as he leaned forward to hand it over, a crackling wave of magic burst through the trees, sizzling straight toward us.

CHAPTER SEVENTEEN

Emeric

Magic lashed against my body, searing my skin and slicing deep. A pained gasp escaped my lips before I could catch it. I hadn't felt a spell so caustic since —since—

Even as I flung myself to the side, instinctively scrambling away from the force of the blast, images from another time flashed through my mind. The scorching sensation, the bolt of agony as the flesh below my right elbow had incinerated. The sight of Dad's crumpled body, blackened from head to chest, limp on the burnt grass of the lawn outside the Nightwood residence.

My heart hammered in my chest, a sweat that had nothing to do with the summer heat breaking over my skin. Where was Cressida? If they'd hurt her…

More energy hissed and flared around us. I caught a glimpse of Cressida's pale braid swinging through the air from the corner of my eye and snatched at her, grasping her elbow.

The Ashwood scion's voice broke through the chaos, ragged but as demanding as yesterday when he'd ordered me to twine my magic with Cressida's. "Get behind a tree! It's only coming from one direction."

I dragged Cressida with me toward the first broad trunk my gaze snagged on. The bark sizzled as another blast of vicious spellwork hit it, but on the other side. The blazing light and heat only streamed around us without reaching us.

Cressida was panting, her face a sickly shade even paler than usual. Without warning, she doubled over and retched at the ground. Nothing came out of her mouth but spit.

Panic gripped my gut. I touched her back, trying to be gentle despite my urgent concern. "Are you all right? Did the magic—"

"It's not the magic," she rasped weakly. "At least not— I was already feeling sick. I think the shock just—" Her voice cut off with another sputter.

She'd barely eaten this morning in front of us. Obviously she hadn't gotten any other food before that, despite her reassurances. I clenched my jaw, berating myself for buying her story. I'd seen how shaky she was getting from time to time as we moved through the woods —I should have asked more questions, done *something*...

Both she and—even I had to admit—the scion had proven themselves to be a hell of a lot more resilient than I'd bet most of the reapers would expect from mages who'd grown up on the posh side of fearmancer society. But we all had limits.

Cressida swiped at her mouth and managed to straighten up, peering at me and then across the woods to the tree several feet away where Noah was crouched. "Are you two okay? Where are the reapers? I didn't know the wards had gone off."

They hadn't, I realized. Even the current bursts of magical energy had petered out, as if faltering now that their intended targets were all out of range. Which didn't make sense, if the reapers had found us. Why wouldn't they keep charging at us?

We'd set wards periodically while we'd been on the move. I murmured a quick casting word and confirmed they were stable, no indication of interference.

"No one's crossed the wards," I said, frowning. But if the reapers hadn't broken through them to attack us, then what the hell had that barrage of magic been?

Noah was rubbing his thigh in a gesture that I recognized in an instant. I'd done something similar enough times with my arm. He was massaging the muscles above the injury as if that could push the pain from below back down. He must have jarred his wounded leg moving out of range.

His voice was still rough when he spoke again. "I think I got a few burns, but I didn't get hit with the full impact where I was sitting, and I didn't have far to go to take shelter. You two were right in the middle of it. You're sure you're all right? You didn't see anything?"

It was totally quiet in the forest other than our low

voices and the rustling of the leaves overhead now. As the rush of my panicked adrenaline faded, stings and aches from across my body crept into my awareness. The skin on my non-titanium forearm was seared raw with a shallow cut down the middle of the burn, seeping blood. From the feel of it, a few patches on the left side of my face were scalded too, as well as my back.

Cressida looked down at her hands, mottled pink burns showing across them and her forearms. The tip of her braid was singed, along with much of her neck. My throat tightened. I'd have offered her a cooling spell to soothe the pain, but the space inside my chest that normally whirled with magic was still unnervingly hollow. I needed to save all the scraps I had left for defending ourselves.

From whatever exactly we were dealing with.

"All I saw were some flares from the magic," I said. "I couldn't make out who was casting the spell."

"Same." Cressida worried at her lip. "I don't hear anything now. They can't have *left*, can they? What the hell is going on?"

My deepest impulse was to run—to put as much distance between us and the threat as I could. But Noah couldn't do more than hobble, and I wasn't sure how fast Cressida could move in her current state. My own body had been feeling increasingly weak from the lack of food and our erratic sleep schedules, not to mention the aftereffects of tearing into my bodily energy to fuel my magic.

Besides, we didn't know where the enemy was. They'd

attacked from one angle, but for all we knew, they could have surrounded us and we'd run right into them. The attack had come from the direction of the town, so if we took off, we'd also be heading away from our goal.

And Lancer—a fresh jolt of fear hit me. I'd left him tucked between the roots of that tree. I didn't sense any injuries through the familiar bond. I tried to picture exactly how I'd left him. He'd been on the safe side of the trunk, right? He was giving off nothing but a faint sense of confusion, which was pretty much status quo since he'd made it back to me.

Noah murmured a few words under his breath. His head swiveled around. "I'm not picking up any human beings anywhere nearby—definitely not close enough to have targeted us like that. It doesn't make any sense…"

Bracing herself, Cressida slowly leaned forward to peek around the tree. At first, nothing happened. She knit her brow, her lips parting as if she was about to speak—and then her braid slipped from her shoulders and swung into view in one swift movement.

Another crackle of magic whipped toward us. Cressida flinched back, and I yanked her to me, holding her for just long enough to confirm she was okay before letting her go, as much as I might have wanted to keep my arms around her.

Just like before, when none of us were provoking it, the magic fell away. "What the fuck?" I muttered.

"There was no one over there," Cressida said, her mouth tensing at a puzzled slant. "Just regular-looking forest." She glanced at me. "I saw Lancer—he's still curled up by that tree. It looked like he's fine."

A strange little pang quavered through me, having her pale eyes locked with mine so close, hearing her attempt at reassurance that she hadn't needed to bother with. I swallowed hard and pulled my gaze away, preparing to take a peek for myself.

An oddly warbled voice broke the stillness of the forest around us, coming from the same direction as the blast of magic. "Traitors and betrayers, you might as well give up now. No matter what you do, where you go, we'll find a way to reach you. Surrender now, and you might still come out of this with your lives."

The voice was too warped for me to recognize who was speaking, but it was clearly one of our pursuers. A chill rippled down my back.

The wards had remained silent. Somehow they were projecting their voice magically to this spot without it triggering our warning spells—somehow they knew exactly where we were—

Understanding struck me, so sharp and cold it took me a few seconds to accept what I could already recognize was true. I pressed my hand to my forehead as if I could jostle free another explanation, but nothing came. The knowledge of what I had to do coiled around my gut with a queasy twist.

"It's my familiar," I said, the words scraping my throat on the way out. "They must have hidden some kind of dormant spell in him with a specific trigger. They knew by now he'd have reached us—they're projecting their spells through him."

Cressida stiffened. "Are you *sure*? You checked him over—"

"If the magic wasn't active, it would have been essentially indetectable. It'll be drawing on his life energy to fuel it now. A bunch of the reapers have been working on perfecting those kind of spells for a while—it's one of their pet projects."

I gritted my teeth for a second, holding back a curse. I'd *known* there was something incredibly odd about Lancer reaching me out in the middle of the forest, but I'd let myself welcome him when there'd been no overt signs of foul play. *I'd* brought this danger into our midst.

And now I had to remove it. I'd sworn an oath to protect the two people with me at all costs. If I resisted, it was my own life on the line—and it wasn't as if losing that would help anyone.

Lance was probably dead either way. The reapers controlling that spell wouldn't stop until they'd drained him to the bone trying to cripple or kill us.

Noah stirred, his gaze seeking out mine. I could tell from his expression that he'd drawn the same conclusion I had, and in that moment, I hated his perceptiveness and the sympathy that carried through in his tone. "There'll be a way to unravel the spell. The barons—the new ones— dealt with things like this before."

"Rory's mentor, Professor Banefield," Cressida said quietly. "When she broke one latent spell, another one kicked in that was even worse. He ended up killing himself, didn't he?"

Noah's momentary silence was answer enough. "There was a contained spell on Connar—on Baron Stormhurst —once. They managed to unravel it without anyone getting hurt."

"How many of them did it take?" I asked. "And was their magic already drained from days wandering in the woods half-starved?" At Noah's hesitation, I grimaced. "Yeah, I didn't think so."

I eased a step back from the tree trunk, studying the forest around me. With some careful maneuvering, I was pretty sure I could dash from shelter to shelter without taking too much damage. And then—

My stomach twisted. I had to do it fast. Both for my familiar's sake and my companions'. Now that the spell in Lancer had activated, the reapers could be tracking him straight to us. In a matter of minutes, we might be dealing with several hostile parties, not just one.

Cressida grabbed my arm. "You don't have to. We could—we could just leave him there, give him a wide berth and circle back around to get the rest of the way to the town. Once we have the barons' help—"

I shook my head, already steeling myself for the task ahead. Every word she said trying to change the situation only made the inevitability of it stab deeper through my chest. "He'll be leading them to us. We don't know what other magic might be on him. They wouldn't let him survive anyway. I *know* this is the only way to really protect you."

Her eyes widened. "That's not—you shouldn't need to —" She swore under her breath, and then her eyes widened as if with an abrupt realization. She sucked in a breath, her fingers squeezing tighter around my wrist. Magic thrummed through her voice. "I, Cressida Warbury, hereby absolve Emeric Riplowe of any and all oaths he's made in regards to my protection."

My pulse stuttered. I could feel part of the pull of the oath fall away, just like that. She'd freed me from every part of the spell that would have ensured my commitment to her safety—to spare me this pain?

As I stared at her, Noah raised his voice from where he was hunched by the other tree. The same power twined through his words. "I, Noah Ashgrave, hereby absolve Emeric Riplowe of any and all oaths he's made in regards to my protection."

The unshakeable tug dissolved completely. I sucked in a hoarse breath, not knowing what to say.

But the truth was, as much as their generosity meant in this moment, as hard as it was for me to believe they'd offered it… it didn't make any difference. We were running out of time. Soon this sacrifice wouldn't be worth anything at all.

"Thank you," I said, my voice coming out slightly choked. "Really. But I still have to do it. I want to see you both make it out of these damned woods with me, oath or not. And I owe it to Lancer not to leave him in those bastards' hands."

Before either of them could protest any further, I jerked my arm free from Cressida's grasp and sprang toward a neighboring tree. A flare of hissing energy shot after me, but it only grazed my back before I'd stumbled behind the shield of the next trunk.

"Emeric," Cressida called after me, sounding miserable, but I didn't look back. I didn't let myself focus on anything but throwing myself toward the next tree and the next, traveling ever closer to the one my familiar was crouched by.

My gaze passed over a stone a little larger than my hand. I paused just long enough to wrap my titanium fingers around it.

I'm sorry, I thought at Lancer, as well as the bearded dragon would be able to understand the sentiment. A gnawing sense of despair was unfurling through my abdomen despite my best attempts to shut down my emotions.

He'd been with me since my first days at Blood U. I'd expected him to have years more by my side.

Cressida was right—our bond *shouldn't* have had to end like this. But it wasn't her fault or the Ashgrave scion's or mine. The assholes I'd allied myself with for reasons that seemed so petty and distant now were the only ones responsible.

And not just for this awfulness. If I really thought about it, who was it who'd brought Dad and me to that battle? Who'd insisted that the upstart scions and their supporters were out to ruin all of fearmancer society, that if we didn't stand up and fight with the current barons, we were as bad as those traitors?

Maybe some of the reapers had honestly believed the

rhetoric, but I'd spent enough time around them to know plenty had only been out to protect their own interests, no matter who else they screwed over. It wasn't hard to imagine that the old barons had been exactly the same way. How could I believe Noah's side was the selfish, ruthless one when he'd just risked his own life in the hopes I could *save* my familiar—the same familiar the reapers had twisted to their ends?

As I came around behind the tree where Lancer was nestled, I intoned a casting word meant to test the spell embedded in his fragile body. A spear of erratic energy bounced right back at me, homing in on my presence, swerving around the tree, and smacking into my face. It scattered my thoughts and left me reeling, braced against the nearest tree trunk.

At the same time, a wave of magic roared from the spot where he sat, hot enough now to char bark and bite into my skin through the air. The trunk at least protected me from the worst of that.

Any shred of hope I might have been holding onto vanished. Just one tentative foray had left me drained. So much intricately twined power had radiated through the backlash that it was hard to conceive of being able to pick the spell on Lancer apart even if I'd been at my best.

The only thing to do was finish this as quickly as possible.

A piercing ache dug deeper into my chest. I closed my eyes for a second, gathering my will, and closed my fingers more firmly around the chunk of rock. *Good-bye, my friend. I wish it didn't have to end this way.*

Then I leapt forward, whipping my titanium arm around the side of the tree to crash down on my familiar's head, exactly where I could sense it lay.

I held the rest of my body as far back as I could, anticipating a different sort of backlash. The second my hand hurtled close to my familiar, a more concentrated blaze of energy sizzled off of him. If I'd attempted this with my other hand, I suspected it'd have been fried to a crisp in an instant.

But either our enemies hadn't considered everything I was made of, or they'd assumed I'd never be willing to go this far to stop them. The enchantments in my titanium arm registered the movement of the air, and a little of the heat trickled as far as the joint where the prosthetic was attached, sending a vicious tingling into my nerves, but nothing stopped the fatal slam of the rock.

Bone crunched. The magic snapped away as if a switch had been flicked. The warmth of the familiar bond blinked out inside me simultaneously. An emptiness so brutal it might as well have been carved by gnashing jaws expanded in its place.

I slumped under the full force of the agony, even more potent than I'd expected. Tears welled up in my eyes. I wheezed for breath, and a second later, Cressida was by my side, gripping my shoulder.

"I'm sorry," she said, sounded choked up herself. "Do you want—I can carry his body…?"

I dragged air into my constricted lungs and managed to heave myself back onto my feet as Noah hopped over to join us. As much as I appreciated the offer, we couldn't risk it. "No, they might have some lesser spells on him that'll help them follow us."

But I wasn't going to leave him for them to dispose of. Murmuring a quick benediction and one final apology, I conjured a spurt of flame across Lancer's limp, bleeding body.

The sight of my familiar crumbling into ash sent another spike of pain through my heart. But it'd been this loss or so much more.

And if I didn't pull myself together, I'd lose everything.

I wrenched my head around to aim my attention toward our goal. "Let's move out before they bring something even worse down on our heads."

CHAPTER EIGHTEEN

Noah

When we stopped in a little glade, I pretended it was only because Emeric and Cressida could cast their spells with more concentration standing still and not at all because they were worried I was about to collapse on my feet. I sank down in the darkest patch of shade I could find, feeling as if liquid fire rather than blood was coursing through my veins. My head spun.

Cressida handed a water bottle to me—hers, I thought, since mine was nearly empty now, but her expression left no room for argument. I pressed it to my forehead, but it was barely cooler than the air. A couple of gulps took the edge off the heat just slightly. Nothing distracted me from the sharper searing emanating up my leg from the trap wound.

Had I jostled it too hard when I'd dodged the spell on Emeric's familiar? Or had the pain been expanding for a while and I'd just managed to deny it until that jarring motion had tipped it over some edge?

Emeric stayed on his feet, but his face had grayed. He pressed his hand to his chest as if trying to hold something in—or push it right out of him.

I'd never had the misfortune of losing a familiar, but it'd happened to one of my classmates in Paris. She'd described the sensation as being like someone had torn a hole right through her ribs. The professors had respected the severity of the situation enough to excuse her from classes for the first couple of days while she recovered.

But our former reaper companion didn't have the luxury of recuperating at his leisure any more than I did. He took a gulp from his own water bottle, smoothed the grimace from his mouth, and turned toward the town we'd been trekking ever closer to.

Cressida was already intoning a quiet casting word. Emeric did as well, either wanting to double-check her observations or figuring he ought to share the responsibility. I'd have liked to offer my own skills, but I could hardly focus well enough to cast another feeble numbing spell on my leg.

The pain retreated a little, but the fever flowing through my body remained just as fiery. Sweat was trickling down the back of my neck just sitting here.

"It's not much farther," Emeric said, the strain twining through his voice. "I think we can make it in an hour or two. Do we want to see if we can get some food into us first or push on right away?"

I opened my mouth to say push on, but Cressida

spoke first. "I think we should at least rest a bit before that last trek. The reapers have probably figured out where we're headed. We won't have as much shelter to hide us going into town, and I don't know how easily we'll find whoever the barons have sent to pick us up. We'll want to be… as fresh as we can be for this last bit." She glanced at Emeric. "Does your phone still have power?"

"It should have a little. I've been keeping it totally off to conserve the battery, and I can juice it up a little magically if I have to." He tapped his pocket. "I was already thinking—I can move the fastest at this point. I'd like to scout out a little ways ahead and see what we might be dealing with and whether I can get a signal to confirm things with the barons. If—if you're okay with me leaving the two of you back here."

His gaze slid from Cressida to me. I looked at him in the slightly bleary way that was the most attention I could pull together at the moment, taking in the stiffness in his stance as he braced himself against whatever internal agony the killing of his familiar had dealt him, the resigned slant of his mouth as if he was fully prepared to accept it if we didn't trust him even this much, even now.

But I did. My fever-hazed mind was sure about that one thing. There'd been no faking the determination with which he'd come to our defense a few hours ago or the sacrifice he'd made. I'd have willingly bet my own familiar's life that Emeric would sooner slaughter every last one of the reapers than rejoin them. Although mostly, at the moment, I suspected he just wanted to reach someplace we could truly rest.

I didn't fully understand why he'd gone along with the reapers for so long or felt justified in coming up with the brutal plan that had brought us here, but I could believe he regretted it with all his being. That there was someone not half bad under the grim defensiveness he'd shown before. Maybe even someone good.

Much of the same sentiments showed on Cressida's face, along with a flicker of what might have been affection. Something twisted in my chest, but I dismissed that flare of jealousy with the closing of my eyes.

She loved me. What more could I possibly ask for? She'd made her peace with how we'd first come together through some inner strength she'd managed to hold onto out here, and she'd shown me how much she wanted to be with me in the clearest way she could. The memories rose up of the taste of her, the feel of her body against mine, the gasps slipping from her mouth…

I blinked, shaking myself out of the reverie, which this definitely wasn't the time for. "I'm fine with you going ahead," I said to Emeric. "You'll definitely cover a lot more ground without waiting on me lurching along."

Cressida shot me a flash of a fond smile and then turned back to Emeric. "Are you sure? You just— I know you can't be feeling all that great right now. If they catch you on your own…"

"They won't," Emeric said firmly. "And if they try, I'll make sure they wish they hadn't." His titanium hand flexed at his side. "I won't take too long. Keep the wards up, and send a signal my way if anyone breaches them."

Cressida opened her mouth and closed it again before

drawing in a rough breath. Her voice came out soft. "It means a lot, what you did for us back there. I never would have expected— You don't have to prove anything else to me. I'm sure it'll take time before I understand everything, but I'm not angry anymore."

Emeric's gaze jerked to her, startled and with a hopeful brightening that was unmistakable. He seemed to rein in those emotions a moment later, but the sight of that intensity, of the hint of a blush that colored Cressida's cheeks in response to it, sent my thoughts rambling in all sorts of directions I hadn't counted on.

"All right," he said gruffly. "Thank you. I'm still going to do everything I can to make sure we all get out of this safely, oath or no."

He nodded to me to include me in that statement, which honestly he hadn't needed to do—and I doubted he cared half as much about my safety as hers. Then he set off with brisk steps and another brush of his hand to his chest.

Cressida came over to me, concern tensing her features. "Did you get enough water? Has Kato managed to find any other food? I could manage a quick cooking spell while Emeric's scouting."

Would she be able to keep anything down? She'd only sipped her water during the last stretch of walking. As I watched her, her legs wobbled before she tensed them.

"Sit down, *mon petite chou-fleur*," I said. "A couple of hours, and we'll have restaurants and cafeterias at our fingertips. I can wait that long."

Her lips twitched with another smile, whether because

of the nickname or my optimism, I couldn't tell. Either way, I'd gotten my desired effect. She sank down onto the earth next to me and leaned her head on my shoulder, careful not to give me too much of her weight.

I lifted my arm, which felt weirdly heavy, and eased it around her shoulders. Being able to openly offer that simple gesture of intimacy sent a giddy thrill through my chest that was totally out of proportion to the act itself. This strong, stubborn, gorgeous girl was *mine*, and no specters of the past could interfere with that now.

The persons very much of our present, well, that was a different story.

I teased my fingers over her hair. "You like him."

She tensed against me. "What?"

"It's fine. I'm just observing. You liked him a lot before you had something to be angry with him about, and now that he's done so much to fix things, it's coming back. I'm sure that's totally normal. I like him too, more than I thought I would. I mean, not *quite* as much as I'm guessing you do, but—"

"Noah," Cressida broke in, pulling away so she could face me properly, and I realized I might have meandered from making conversation into babbling. She gazed into my eyes so intently my heart skipped a beat. "Yes, I was interested in him before. Yes, there are reasons it wouldn't be ridiculous for me to feel that way again. But you don't have to worry about— I'm with *you*. I want to be with you. I'm *happy* with you. I'm not going to throw that away."

It took me a little while to sort out why she thought

she had to reassure me so much. The brief pang of jealousy seemed very distant now.

I reached for her hand and squeezed it. "That's not what I meant. I was only thinking—maybe it doesn't have to be either/or. If there's something about him that makes you happy too, then you could have twice the happiness, or close to it."

The way she was staring at me made me wonder if I'd suddenly started speaking French without noticing. But apparently not, because then she let out a startled laugh and said, "Are you seriously saying you wouldn't mind if I —if I dated him, or whatever, too? *Encouraging* me to do that, even?"

I shrugged, which left my thoughts whirling for a few seconds before I could concentrate on what I'd intended to say again. "Declan manages to share Rory with three other guys. I think I can handle one."

A snort that appeared to surprise even Cressida sputtered out of her. Her tone turned wry. "So this is actually about proving you can be at least as good as your brother in every possible way?"

Was it? I hadn't considered that, but her point might have factored in a little. But by far the biggest part was—"I love you, and I want you to be happy. As happy as possible. That's all."

"Noah…" I couldn't tell what she was thinking, but something about the conversation had brought a glow into her face so bright I could have basked in it for the rest of my life. At least, I could have if my vision hadn't started to go fuzzy around the edges.

She raised her hand to my cheek and abruptly jerked it back. "You're burning up. Are you feeling worse?"

It was getting increasingly hard to focus enough to form answers. "I think—it has been very hot."

She touched my cheek again and then my forehead, her breath hissing out of her. "That's got to be a fever—it feels like a bad one. You need to stay hydrated. Have some more of the water. I'll splash some on your forehead."

Her tone was turning frantic. I opened my mouth to tell her that we shouldn't waste the water we still had left pouring it on my face, but somewhere between my brain and my tongue I lost the thought.

A sharper rush of heat washed over me, flipping my mind right over, and my grip on the world around me splintered away.

CHAPTER NINETEEN

Cressida

Noah slumped over, his head lolling. My heart lurched. I caught him before he hit the ground, shuddering at how limp his body felt. And how hot. The heat of his fever wafted into my arms where I held him.

Why hadn't I noticed how flushed he was looking? I had—I'd just assumed it was the exertion of the walk and the thickening heat of the day. Fuck. Was his leg infected? How bad was it if he was this spaced out?

Terms like "blood poisoning" and "sepsis" flashed through my mind. People *died* from untreated infections. And Noah's wound had been left without proper medical attention for days.

What the hell did I do? He couldn't even walk now…

I propped him as well as I could against the tree he'd been sitting by so I didn't have to cling onto him to keep him from falling. Then I patted his cheeks, as firmly as I dared. "Noah. Noah, can you stay awake? Noah!"

His eyelids fluttered. They opened briefly, his gaze wandering dazedly without appearing to see me at all. Then his eyes drifted shut again.

I inhaled sharply. It didn't matter how much danger we were in from the reapers. We had to get him to the barons' people quick, or we might lose him without the reapers setting one finger on him.

I was just spinning around to conjure some signal for Emeric when footsteps rustled through the forest. He came into view a moment later, frowning—a frown that deepened when he took in my expression.

He hurried the rest of the way to the glade. "What's wrong?"

I gestured frantically to Noah. "I think his leg must have gotten infected. He has a horrible fever, and he fainted—I can't get him to really wake up."

Emeric swore and dropped to a crouch at Noah's side. It was strange seeing the intense attention with which he checked the other guy's forehead and murmured a few casting words that must have been from his limited medical training. A few days ago, he'd barely wanted to look at the Ashgrave scion, let alone offer him any help.

A lot of things had changed during this unexpected journey.

Kato came scrambling out of the deeper woods just then. The raccoon leapt straight to his master, patting Noah's hair with his dainty paws as if he could help too.

When Noah didn't react, his familiar let out a distressed grunt.

"We're trying everything we can," I told him, as if he'd understand.

After a minute, Emeric glanced up at me with his forehead furrowed and an apology in his tone. "Nothing I'm trying is bringing the fever down. I don't want to unbandage his leg—there probably isn't anything I could do for an infection this bad anyway, and it might open up the wound. We've got to get him to someone who actually knows what they're doing."

"I know," I said. "But *how?*"

My own legs wavered under me, and not just because of my panic. My stomach was roiling again, the unsteadiness that'd been creeping over me since I'd first started feeling sick tightening its hold. My hands itched to reach for Noah, to whisk him to safety, but I doubted I could carry even half his weight right now, let alone support him completely.

Emeric's gaze took in my state. He didn't comment on my weakness, just nodded. "We'll manage. The real problem is the reapers. They laid down some kind of magical snare all along the edge of the forest at the outskirts of town. I don't have anywhere near enough power to try to untangle it. I'm not even sure exactly what it'll do if we walk into it, other than I doubt it'll be *good*."

A chill wrapped around me. "And who knows what else they have waiting for us other than that."

"I did manage to talk to Baron Ashgrave for a couple of minutes. Not the greatest signal, but he said there's a team of blacksuits—ones loyal to them, not the reapers—in town waiting for us. The problem is that as soon as we alert them any obvious way, the reapers will see it too."

"And if there's still some magical trap between us and the blacksuits, we're screwed." I rubbed my forehead. "Okay. There has to be something we can do. Let's—let's get to the point where we can detect the snare, and I'll see what I can make of it." I wasn't sure I'd be able to come up with any strategy that Emeric wouldn't, but two minds had to be at least a little better than one.

Without another word, Emeric eased Noah off the ground. The scion hadn't been the beefiest guy to begin with, and a week without proper food had started to thin him out even more. It didn't look as if it took too much effort for Emeric to sling the other guy over his shoulder, adjusting Noah carefully so he'd be stable.

"Okay," he said. "I think I can get him there. It's not too far."

I snatched up his pack, even though we might not need anything in it after this last trek. We set off, Emeric managing to walk faster than me through the brush even with his much heavier cargo. Kato bounded along beside us, never letting Noah out of his sight. Percy swooped closer through the trees, sensing my own distress.

After several minutes, Emeric slowed, holding up his hand in a signal for us to stay as quiet as possible. We slunk between the trees for another short distance. Then he stopped completely. Noah stirred with a brief mumbling, but as Emeric shifted his weight, the scion fell silent again.

My throat tight, I whispered a casting word for testing the presence of magic and threw it off my tongue toward the terrain ahead. It only took a few seconds before an impression of a massive spell rippled back to me. A wall of energy, prickling and quivering, lay ahead of us.

But beyond the treetops, I could make out the spire of a church steeple in the near distance. We were *so* close.

I wet my lips. "You'd assume that the spell will activate if we walk into it, right? It'll trap us somehow."

"That'd be my best guess," Emeric said. "It has a… grasping sort of feeling to it."

Now that he'd said it, I could see what he meant. I dragged in a breath. "Okay." My weary mind pinged from one possibility to another, each seeming even more hopeless than the last. And the longer we stood here, the more chance there was that the reapers would notice us and catch us without even using their damned spell.

But we couldn't just run in throwing caution to the wind. Our last mad dash had been what'd left Noah with that wound.

The memory of the trap snapping shut around Noah's leg sent a shudder through me—and a spark of inspiration.

I rolled the idea around in my head for a few seconds, but my enthusiasm only flared brighter. "What if… What if we could trigger their trap somehow before we actually get there? Once it closes around *something*, it shouldn't affect us if we make a run for it, don't you think?"

Emeric grimaced. "Sure, but they must have set it so only a person will trigger it. Maybe even a person with some kind of magical element to their presence. They wouldn't want it going off for squirrels or sparrows or even a random Nary wandering into the woods. For all we know, they have some of your and Noah's blood from when you were at the Kingsleys', and it's keyed to that."

"Right." I glanced around us, thinking of how many ways we'd already made use of the natural materials of the forest: leaves for bedding, stones for bowls, moss for bandages. Maybe we had everything we needed right here around us.

"An illusion isn't going to help us with that," I said. "But—do you think you have enough power to shape some earth and leaves and whatever else works into something decently human-shaped? Something you can make walk?"

Emeric's eyebrows leapt up, but he didn't refuse. "Like some kind of golem," he said.

"Yeah. Three of them. We can add a bit of blood to them, and they'll have magic animating them... It might be enough to spring the trap."

He set Noah down gently at the base of a tree and murmured another quick spell over the other guy. Seeing Noah's body lying there so limply sent a fresh jolt of urgency through me. I bit my lip while Emeric considered the situation in silence.

Finally, he inclined his head. "I think I can manage it. It'll take a lot out of me—I'm not sure how much else I'll be useful for after that—but if I use lighter materials like leaves, it won't take *too* much energy to propel them forward. We'd want them to cross over pretty far from where we're going to make our dash, though, or the reapers will run into us while they're hurrying to retrieve the contents of their trap."

It was late enough in the afternoon that the shadows were stretching long. I mentally prodded my own dwindled stores of magic. "Yeah. I can cast some shadows and other impressions around us to make us less visible too."

"All right." Emeric looked at Noah's slumped form, and his jaw tensed. "Let's get to it."

While I conjured fragments of shadow along with a reflective illusion that would echo the vegetation around us rather than our forms, Emeric began intoning his own spells. One after another, he built three person-like shapes into being out of leaves and grass like he'd once sculped animals out of ocean water. At his direction, they shuffled awkwardly across the uneven ground.

Watching them, I shivered. Even without any details like eyes or fingers, there was something incredibly eerie about them.

But hey, it'd been my idea. And I had to see it all the way through. I murmured a small nick into being on my thumb and smeared a streak of blood down the back of one of the forms, restraining a cringe. With a quiet apology, I stole a little of Noah's blood for the same purpose.

Once Emeric had doctored his, he hefted Noah over his shoulders again. His expression looked taut, his skin yellowed, but he stood steadily enough that I only worried a little.

"Okay," he said. "Here goes nothing. We don't know how much time we'll have before they figure out the trick. You're ready to run?"

I nodded. "Just head to the town as fast as you can. Don't wait for me if I can't quite keep up." If I faltered and the reapers grabbed me, at least the two guys could hopefully evade them.

Emeric sent his animated figures tramping off at a diagonal from us. Their rustling steps carried through the forest as we slunk closer to the snare spell ourselves. Emeric's face had gone rigid with concentration. I watched him, waiting for the sign that he was ready to launch our plan.

He lifted his hand as if to say, *Almost*. His eyes narrowed. He spoke a few syllables under his breath. Then with one final word, he made a jerky gesture toward me and lunged forward as fast as he could go while carrying Noah.

At the same moment, energy warbled through the brush, powerful enough to stir a wind that grazed my face. But it was whipping away from us, toward the spot where Emeric must have sent his leafy golems to barge into the trap.

I sprinted forward as fast as my wobbly legs could take me across the unpredictable forest floor, my gaze fixed on Emeric's back and Noah's body slung over his shoulders ahead of me. Just keep moving, just keep putting one foot after the other... I'd have all the time in the world to collapse when it wouldn't cost me my life.

Within moments, every muscle in my body was

burning—but the trees thinned up ahead. I made out a car whizzing along a road and the sprawl of small-town buildings beyond it. My pulse hiccupped with excitement.

We hurtled across the last stretch of woodland so fast I barely felt the ground beneath my feet. Emeric's breath came short and ragged, but a smile touched his lips. As we burst from the forest and leapt the ditch at the side of the road, my mind scrambled to come up with a clear enough illusion that would catch the blacksuits' attention and bring them to us without breaking the rules about allowing Naries to witness magic.

As a car roared nearer, we braced to charge across the second it'd passed by—and the shriek of another vicious spell careened toward us.

CHAPTER TWENTY

Cressida

I didn't let myself stop to look for the spell's caster or to see if I could discern anything about its purpose. Whatever it was, the sound of it alone was enough to tell me it wasn't good.

Ignoring the car zooming toward us, I flung myself across the road with all the strength I had left in me.

Tires screeched. Emeric pounded after me. The wave of magic whipped by with a numbing lash across my back, but it only grazed my skin.

We stumbled down the ditch on the opposite side, a cramped bit of shelter. Percy soared by overhead; Kato slid down next to us. More spells hissed by over our heads. My heart battered my ribs as I struggled to catch my breath.

There was a long stretch of pavement to the nearest building, what looked to be an elementary school on the edge of town. It was late enough in the day that the yard was mostly deserted, thank god, but a couple of older kids were riding their bikes in circles between us and the building.

I'd have hoped their presence—hell, even the presence of the cars still rumbling by—would be enough to dissuade the reapers, but the whole battle between them and the new barons had been about them wanting to use their magic openly to dominate the Naries. *They* didn't give a shit about exposure.

We'd be easy targets darting across that space—but we were increasingly at risk the longer we stayed in one spot too. I urged my familiar farther into town where he wouldn't draw our attackers to our exact location. *Look for blacksuits. Look for university-type people,* I thought at him, hoping he'd at least get the gist of those instructions.

I glanced over at Emeric, who was still clutching Noah's slack body as carefully as he could, and a trickle of despair threatened to spread through my chest.

We'd made it this far, but we were both so drained after that final dash.

If I could have used the same trick I had in the woods before, making it look like we were running in a different direction, that might have bought us enough time. It was still daylight even if the sun was sinking, though, and there were no trees to obscure the details of our forms here. I'd have to make the illusions convincing. It took a lot out of a mage to create even *one* convincing illusion of a human being, let along three…

Why had I ever thought I could take on all our enemies? I should have stayed at Blood U and forgotten any delusions of repaying the barons for accepting me.

That thought passed through my head, and a surge of defiance rose up to meet it. *No.* I was not giving up—I was going to give this bid for safety my all. I might not be a spectacular mage, but I was a pretty damn good illusionist. If there'd ever been a time to stretch my abilities to the limit, this was it.

And if I needed to play traitor one more time to get the energy I needed to win the battle, so be it.

Without giving myself a chance to second-guess the strategy, I let my eyes narrow, staring Emeric down. I forced an edge into my voice. "I don't think we're both going to make it," I said, raising my hand as if to cast a caustic spell of my own straight at him.

Even though I'd wanted the effect, it hurt a little to see how quickly and sharply his fear jolted into me. Some part of him truly believed that after everything, I might be the kind of person who'd kill him to save my own skin. But self-preservation was the strongest of all instincts, and human fear fueled a mage like nothing else. The energy flooding into me gave me a rush no startled bird or rodent had been able to offer anything even close to.

After being close to drained for so long, the sudden, potent influx was giddying. I didn't have time to revel in it, though. I yanked my gaze from Emeric's widening eyes and focused my mind on my appearance as I'd seen it so many times in the mirror, on Emeric's and Noah's as we'd tramped together through the woods.

With emphatic syllables I rolled off my tongue, I threw all the energy I'd gathered from him into conjuring images to match a hundred feet away, scrambling out of the ditch.

I couldn't afford to spend much time directing the illusions, so I simply sent them on a course charging straight on a diagonal away from us and hoped they'd hold their form for long enough to buy us the rest of our escape. I didn't even have the chance to admire the most impressive work I'd ever accomplished. As magic whined through the air in the distance toward those fake figures, I grasped Emeric's titanium forearm and yanked him toward the schoolyard.

Thankfully, he wasn't so distracted by my fake threat that he'd failed to realize I didn't actually intend to slaughter him. Just like that, he was up and running, hefting Noah to balance the other guy across his shoulders.

We sprinted toward the school building, giving the kids as wide a berth as we could. One of them let out a startled shout, but I didn't let my focus waver from the squat brick building up ahead. A tremor rippled through the muscles in my legs. Just a little farther—just a little—

Less than ten steps from the shadow cast by the school, my calves gave out. I pitched forward, scraping my palms and knees on the dimpled concrete. Emeric kept going on momentum, but the second he made it to the corner of the building, he spun around. I staggered upright, wincing and waving for him to keep going.

He waited anyway, reaching to grasp my elbow the

second I was close enough—which turned out to be a good thing, because he yanked me past the shelter of the wall just as a spell crackled at my heels.

The jig was up. The reapers had spotted the real us.

Where the hell were the blacksuits who were supposed to be coming to our rescue?

Ignoring the searing sensation filling my lungs, I hurried onward next to Emeric. My voice came out raspy. "We have to find… someplace secure… or at least kind of secure… where I can cast something to signal the blacksuits."

He nodded, his head swiveling to take in the street beyond the school. "Over there," he said, equally hoarse, pointing to the church with the spire I'd spotted where it stood at the end of a busy street. The door hung open, and we should blend in a little with the other pedestrians as we made our way over.

We hustled along, crossing the street and staying close to the storefronts so passersby would shield us from view. We must have stuck out like sore thumbs with our rumpled, dirty clothes, a raccoon scampering along at our heels, and Noah so obviously out of it, even more so in a small town like this. Several people paused and stared as we rushed by—a few tried to ask if we needed help, but I tossed out quick thank yous and reassurances without stopping.

We did need help, but not anything the Naries could offer. Even lingering in their company would put them in the line of fire.

As the church loomed closer, I murmured a quick casting word, fixing my gaze on the tufts of clouds gliding by overhead. More illusionary wisps gathered together until they formed a symbol like the dragon's head emblem for Blood U, drifting down to settle over the spire.

That'd better be clear enough to catch the blacksuits' attention. Percy reached out to me with a whiff of curiosity, and for good measure, I encouraged him to circle the emblem. None of the regular people around us appeared to have noticed it, but I doubted it'd take much time for our pursuers to spot it. How long did I have to leave it up there to be sure of our rescue?

It didn't seem to matter, because the reapers were already on our tail. Behind us, someone yelped as a sizzling streak of magic flew along the street. My chest hitched, but Emeric was already spitting out a spell of his own. The hostile energy crashed into an invisible shield he'd thrown up around us.

We weren't such a bad team when he wasn't screwing me over and I wasn't attempting to terrify him.

We pushed ourselves faster, Emeric's grip on my elbow tightening when I swayed. He couldn't very well carry me too. Clenching my jaw, I willed my legs to hold out just a little longer. *When you make it back to Blood U, you can rest for days. Weeks. I'll even give you* years *if you just carry me the rest of the way to that church.*

Dodging traffic, we dashed across the street and up the front steps to the church's arched doorway. I caught sight of a few people sitting in the pews way down by the altar before I ducked to the side into the empty vestibule just inside the door.

As I dropped to the cool tiled floor, my back against the wall, Emeric sank down beside me. He eased Noah off his shoulders and lay him down, tucking the scion's arm beneath his head to cushion it. Kato curled up beside him.

"Now we just wait and see who gets here first?" he said, a thread of dark humor running through his weary voice.

I sputtered a laugh. "Something like that. You want to try getting Declan on the phone again?"

Emeric grimaced. "Battery's dead now. I don't think I have enough magic to juice it up properly again."

The memory of how I'd boosted *my* stores of magic just minutes ago came back to me with a prickle of regret. Without thinking, I grabbed his hand, the real one, and squeezed it. "I'm sorry—about earlier. It was the only way I could think of to quickly—"

He'd looked startled as my fingers had closed around his, but he recovered fast enough to cut me off, gripping my hand tightly in return. "It's okay. You did what you had to do. I'd rather be scared for my life for a few seconds than actually lose it."

My lips twitched with a smile at his tone. It faltered as a hum of energy from beyond the walls tingled over my skin. *Someone* was coming, seeking us out. I suspected it wasn't the company we wanted.

I inhaled deeply, readying myself for one last standoff. "We'll get through this. Just like the scions overcame the barons. Just like I got away from my parents. The bullies don't have to win if we don't let them. I'm not ready to stop fighting yet."

Emeric looked down at our joined hands. Some emotion passed over his face that I couldn't read. Then, without warning, he leaned in to bring his mouth to mine.

It was a swift kiss, a brief press of heat and determination and then over. Not so much a romantic act as a simple reminder that we were still alive. My pulse skipped a beat all the same. But before I could figure out how I wanted to respond, another shriek of magical energy split the air outside.

I tensed up, pulling the first casting words I could think of onto my tongue. Then there was a sputtering sound and a shudder of breeze, and several footsteps thumped up the church steps.

I'd already leapt up into a defensive position when my mind registered the black slacks and collared shirts all of the figures wore: the blacksuits' standard uniform.

Relief washed over me so abruptly I nearly keeled right over with it. One woman stepped toward us, her jaw going slack as she took us in. "Miss Warbury? And—"

Her gaze dropped to Noah, and she sprang forward. "The Ashgrave scion needs medical attention!"

Three of her colleagues had stationed themselves in the doorway. Two others hurried over to check Noah. My heart beat out a heavy rhythm against my ribs, knowing the worst might not be over yet. "His leg got gouged up pretty badly—he turned feverish sometime today. We think it must be infected."

They were already muttering spells and easing Noah

up off the floor between two of them. The woman motioned to Emeric and me. "We'll get you all out of here. We sent the van around the back. Come on, before the people after you have a chance to make any more trouble."

I couldn't argue with that.

I scooped up Kato, and we hustled down a side passage through the church and emerged into the waning daylight to find a large black van stopped with the engine still running just a few feet from the back door. The blacksuits ushered us into the back, where benches lined the side walls. The two who'd carried Noah laid him on the floor while continuing to intone spells over him. Kato immediately leapt down beside him.

The doors slammed, magic crackled somewhere beyond the steel frame, and the vehicle lurched into motion.

We were going. We were leaving the woods and the reapers behind. I couldn't see Percy, but I could feel him soaring after us. I stared through the hazily tinted window in disbelief, part of me braced for some blast of magic to rock the van off its wheels.

But the town fell away behind us, the open road stretching ahead, and gradually the sense crept over me that it really was over.

A choking sensation filled my throat. Then Noah stirred, his eyes opening to fix blearily on my face. He shifted as if to reach for me, but the blacksuits held him in place. "What's wrong, *chou-fleur*?" he mumbled, not quite himself but more with us than he'd been a half hour ago.

Tears burned behind my eyes, and a smile stretched across my face that I couldn't restrain. "Nothing," I said. "Nothing's wrong. We're all right now."

No matter what I'd said to Emeric, I wasn't sure I'd truly believed we would make it until right this moment.

CHAPTER TWENTY-ONE

Cressida

The warm late-August breeze licked over the grass on the university green with a peaceful rustling sound, but I eyed the lawn with trepidation, keeping my feet planted firmly on the stone step outside Killbrook Hall. The greenery was a far cry from the woods beyond the Kingsleys' chalet, but the sound and the color took me back in an instant. The memory of bright leaves swaying overhead and a hopeless sensation wrapped around my gut swept through me.

I shook it off with a half-hearted grimace. "I think I've been traumatized by all things nature-y. Can't we find somewhere to live that has no vegetation?"

Noah, who'd stopped beside me on our way out of the building, slung his arm around my shoulders. The casual affection in the gesture—the fact that he offered that affection so easily—still sparked a disbelieving giddiness in my chest.

"Already planning for us to move in together, huh?" he teased. "I mean, it's a little fast, but I'm up for it if you are."

Heat flared in my cheeks. "That's not what I meant," I retorted, jabbing him lightly with my elbow.

"Hey, no beating up the invalid. Who'll come to my rescue now?"

I rolled my eyes toward him, taking more pleasure than I let myself show in seeing the healthy color in his own cheeks, the alert gleam in his deep brown eyes.

Noah had spent most of our first week back on campus in the university's health center, getting his body cured of its infection, his wounded leg healed, and his half-starved body re-nourished. But by halfway through that time, he'd been talking with all his usual energy, and now another week had passed since the medical staff had pronounced him perfectly healthy.

"You can't play that card anymore, na-vet," I informed him.

He laughed at the new nickname I'd picked out for him with the assistance of an online French dictionary and ever-so-helpfully corrected my pronunciation. "It's na-*veh*."

"Whatever, turnip," I muttered, tucking myself more closely against his lean frame. "You'd better watch out. I'm going to come up with a whole list that are *so* much better than 'cauliflower'."

Noah chuckled again and kissed my temple. "Ah, you love being my *petit chou-fleur*."

I did, very much, even if I wasn't going to admit it at this exact moment.

I hadn't had much time yet to enjoy the fact that I loved… well, everything about being with him. The medical staff had watched over my own recovery, though with not quite the intense scrutiny they'd dedicated to the soon-to-be baron, and then I'd thrown myself into scrambling to catch up with my classes despite Rory's assurances that I wouldn't be penalized for the missed work. It'd been hectic but fantastically *normal* feeling, which'd been a nice change of pace.

But summer term had ended a few days ago, and most of even the students avid enough to attend those classes for extra credits had headed home for their week off before our regular studies resumed in September. I'd stuck around like I always did, because I had nowhere else to go, and Noah had stayed on campus rather than relax at any of the Ashgrave residences… possibly so he could stay with me.

With no dormmates around to comment, we'd spent the past few nights together, alternating between his room and mine. I was still discovering just how joyful sex could be with someone I completely wanted who seemed to adore me in return, who took as much delight in seeing me happy as satisfying himself. But really, my favorite moments were waking up next to him in the cozy comfort of an actual bed, seeing that he was still there, peaceful and unharmed. Remembering that we'd made it out of hell and somehow come together at the same time.

There was something miraculous about that fact, but thinking about the approaching fall term and its influx of students made my stomach knot.

"People are going to talk, you know," I said. "A scion dating the daughter of two of the most prominent enemies of the current barony?"

Noah shrugged without shifting his arm from my shoulders. "So they'll talk. There's always something. Anyone who has doubts about my choice clearly doesn't know you at all."

He spoke with so much certainty that my nerves settled. People had *always* talked about me, so I wasn't worried on my own behalf.

I was about to suggest we head into town for the rest of the afternoon—to get away from any forest-like imagery for a bit—but just then a familiar well-built form strode into view from the direction of the health center.

Since the blacksuits had picked us up in Jondale, Emeric had been staying at the university too. Going back to his home in Portland wasn't exactly safe, and he probably preferred being close to his sister, who'd no doubt become a target for the reapers if she left the campus. The jerks did have a thing for revenge.

As far as I knew, Emeric had recovered just fine from the traumas of our trek—both physical and emotional— although it'd sounded like his connection to his prosthetic arm had become disrupted. Maybe the medical staff were still working on that with him.

We hadn't really talked since we'd gotten here. I'd been busy with classwork and then Noah, and I'd gotten the sense Emeric was giving me a wide berth. Which made sense. I might have forgiven him while our lives were on the line and we kind of *had* to depend on each other, but he probably wasn't sure of his reception now that the threat was gone.

He hesitated at the edge of the green when he saw us and then gave us a careful nod in greeting. I thought his gaze lingered for a moment on Noah's arm around me. Then he started walking again, on a course that would take him past us to one of the hall's other entrances.

Noah leaned in so his lips brushed the shell of my ear. "We *could* give people even more to talk about, you know."

I glanced over at him, surprise and a bit of a thrill shooting through me. The memory of Emeric's brief kiss in the church flickered through my mind with a tingle of heat. I'd assumed—it'd been *easier* to assume—that Noah hadn't really meant what he'd said that afternoon about sharing. He'd been out of his mind with the fever. But the suggestiveness of his tone now indicated otherwise.

"You remember saying all that?" I asked. "I figured it was the fever talking."

He hummed. "I'll admit I wasn't exactly in my right mind at the time, but I think that only helped me draw the conclusions I did faster—and say them out loud. My mind hasn't changed. And my temperature is currently perfectly fine."

Raising my eyebrows at him, I touched his forehead

just to confirm. The gleam in his eyes had turned sly. "It was only an idea," he added. "The decision is obviously yours. I'm just letting you know that if you *wanted* to explore the possibilities, I'm on board."

I turned the idea over in my head, my gaze sliding back to Emeric's broad-shouldered form crossing the green. I *had* forgiven him, fully and truly—and in a weird way, I'd kind of missed having him so close at hand over the past two weeks. Thinking of the way he'd offered a sort of blessing to my relationship with Noah, of the passion in his voice when he'd mentioned the feelings for me he hadn't been able to shut out, another flare of warmth flowed through my veins.

We'd had something, even if it hadn't been totally real, those moments in Portland when we'd gotten close. And we'd had something again, fraught and raw but honest, by the time we'd left the woods behind. I wasn't sure exactly what I wanted, but maybe it was time I found out.

I eased forward, reaching to grab Noah's hand as it slipped to my side, and called out before the other guy reached the doorway. "Emeric!"

He halted, looking over at us with a startled expression he reeled in a moment later. "Yes?" he said tentatively.

It felt ridiculous trying to have a conversation across half the green. It felt pretty ridiculous having this conversation at all, but I'd committed now. I walked over, Noah falling into step beside me, so I didn't have to raise my voice. That also gave me a chance to grope for the right way to start.

I motioned vaguely toward Ashgrave Hall. "We've

hardly seen each other since—since everything. Maybe we could… catch up? I've got my whole dorm to myself. We could hang out in the common room."

Emeric studied me and then Noah for a few beats, as if evaluating our intentions. Did he think this was some kind of ambush? I guessed in a way it was, though I doubted it was the type he'd be considering. I smiled, hoping it looked friendly and not awkward, and something softened in his eyes that sent another of those tingles of warmth through me.

He scratched the back of his neck with his gloved hand—he'd gone back to wearing them to hide his prosthetic now that we were in larger society again. "All right. Lead the way."

The vibe between us didn't exactly get less awkward as we headed into the residence building and up the stairs. When I let the guys into my dorm, it occurred to me that I hadn't been planning on playing host. I had a bottle of Icelandic vodka stashed in the back of the fridge, but getting even tipsy while navigating a potentially precarious negotiation seemed like a very bad idea. It definitely hadn't gotten Noah and me off to the best start.

I waved for the guys to sit down in the lounge area and checked to see what else we had on hand. "Do you want anything to drink? There's, er, water, and I've got some orange juice and a couple of Cokes." The Cokes technically belonged to one of my dormmates, but I could replace them before she got back.

Noah sprawled out at one end of the sofa, stretching his legs to the base of the coffee table. "I'll take a Coke."

Emeric contemplated the layout and took an armchair near the opposite end of the sofa. "Just tap water is fine for me. I've developed a new appreciation for it."

An unexpected laugh tumbled out of me. "No kidding. I promise no algae or silt in this stuff."

Something about that exchange broke the ice. When I returned to the lounge area carrying glasses of water for Emeric and me—because I had to say I savored the tap water a hell of a lot more than I'd used to too—and Noah's Coke, Emeric had settled into the chair in a more relaxed pose. I set the drinks down on the table, and he left his there, watching us.

"You've both been all right?" he asked, and focused on Noah. "I know they had you in the health center for a while."

Noah grinned. "More because they feared my older brother thinking they weren't doing enough for me than because I needed that much coddling."

I glowered at him. "You almost *died*."

"Well, they fixed *that* part within a day. The rest was just extra fussing."

I turned back to Emeric. "They cast some treatments on me, but it didn't seem like anything major was wrong. I was back here by the next day. How about you? I heard there was some problem with your arm…"

If it was a sensitive subject, he didn't show any discomfort. "It's not responding to my mental signals quite as well as it used to. The best we've been able to figure, it was something about the spell that came out of Lancer when—when I had to put him down."

The corners of his mouth twitched downward with that recollection. He collected himself. "I've been going in every couple of days to run through some exercises, and it's improving. I'm almost back to where it was before."

"That's good," I said, meaning it. I didn't think the battle where he'd lost his arm could have gone much differently without far worse consequences, but I still didn't like the idea of him continuing to struggle after all the other personal consequences he'd already faced.

"You went back to Portland briefly with a blacksuit escort, didn't you?" Noah said, which must have been information he'd heard from the barons. "Were you able to get everything you needed?"

Emeric nodded, another shadow crossing his expression. "I'd already moved the most important things to a safe space no one else knew about in case the whole plot went sideways one way or another. Someone trashed my house while we were away, but nothing I can't live without was taken or destroyed. It's not exactly livable anymore, though… It looks like Shauna and I will be relying on the university's hospitality for a while until I can get back on my feet."

And until he didn't have to worry about the reapers assassinating either of them the second they stepped outside these wards unprotected, he didn't have to add.

"I'm sure Ms. Grimsworth doesn't mind." My mouth slanted into a crooked smile. "She's tolerated me hanging around for the past two years."

I still didn't know where I was going to end up after I graduated at the end of next term, but that question no longer weighed on me quite so heavily. After what I'd already survived, it was hard to worry much about problems like finding the perfect job.

"She's been very tolerant so far," Emeric acknowledged. "More than I would have expected."

The hint of self-doubt in his tone made my throat tighten. Suddenly it felt vital that I establish one thing right off the bat. "You were in a bad place, and you made bad decisions, but that's not—that's not all of who you are, and people here understand that. The ones who count the most, anyway."

A hint of a flush colored his face. "You don't have to make excuses for me."

"That's not what I'm doing. You have no idea… *I* did some horrible things while I still had my parents' ideas crowding out everything else, and I'd never lost anything or anyone on the same level you had to justify all that hostility. I'm not suggesting that what you did was okay, but I get it. You said you'd be happy as long as I didn't see you as an enemy by the time we made it back here. Well, I don't, if you had any doubts about that."

Emeric blinked at me, and then a warmer light came into his cool eyes. "So you didn't bring me back here to kill me after all," he said in a cautiously joking tone.

I found myself grinning back. "Oh, if that was what I had in mind, I'd have come up with a much better plan than this. You're safe for now."

He leaned forward and held out his hand. "Friends, then?" The wariness in his expression hadn't totally gone away, as if he was still preparing for me to reject him.

I grasped his hand to give it a quick shake, feeling the firmness of his titanium fingers through the soft leather. That sensation and the flash of longing he couldn't quite disguise reminded me of the first time he'd touched me with that hand ungloved, tracing his metal fingertips over my cheek. Of watching him in the chilly ocean water, conjuring sea creatures for my entertainment.

Of the loneliness, grief, and nobility I'd caught glimpses of then and during our trek through the forest.

I was happy with Noah, absolutely. But he hadn't been wrong. Some part of me was drawn to something in Emeric too… and maybe I should give that connection a chance as well. Give myself the chance to see just how happy I could be.

If Emeric had earned a real second chance, then surely by now I had as well.

I let go of his hand, but a quiver of electricity remained in the air between us. It took me a second to catch my breath. Then I pushed the words out before I could chicken out. "What if I want to be more than friends?"

There was no missing the hope and hunger that crossed Emeric's face in the moment before he reined those emotions in. He stared at me, and Noah, and then me again. "I… I thought the two of you…"

"We are," Noah said with a broad smile. "But it turns out I'm the generous type."

I swatted him. "It seems to run in his family," I said to Emeric. "You know Rory Bloodstone is with Declan Ashgrave *and* three of the other barons."

He was still staring. I fumbled for the right thing to say.

"I— We had something, didn't we—before? You told me you weren't really faking it when it was just the two of us getting to know each other. There were a lot of things I liked about that guy, and there was more that I saw that I can admire in the one who got us through those woods no matter what it cost you. So maybe… Maybe if Baron Bloodstone can date four guys at once, it's not totally impossible that I could make it work with two. I mean, if you could accept that."

Emeric still looked uncertain. "I don't know. I never really thought…"

My stomach sank. I managed another smile, tighter this time. Of course he hadn't. He probably thought *I* was ridiculous. Why had I let Noah talk me into this?

"It's all right," I said quickly. "I didn't mean to put you on the spot. You don't have to decide anything right now —and I won't be offended if you say no whenever you do decide. I know it's an unusual suggestion, and—"

Emeric pushed himself off of the chair, the sudden movement startling me silent. His eyes flashed. "Fuck it," he said, and leaned in to kiss me.

It was a real kiss this time, not the brief peck from the church. His mouth captured mine as if staking a claim, urgent and wanting, and my whole body shivered eagerly in response.

We'd been through so much, had so much faith shaken and shattered, but somehow we'd rebuilt it, and this moment felt like some kind of homecoming.

Noah let out a rough sound, and my pulse stuttered at the thought that the reality of seeing another man kissing me might have been harder to take than whatever he'd imagined. But before I could pull back to make sure he was all right, he'd scooted closer to me on the sofa, his hand tracing the curve of my thigh through my jeans and his lips marking the crook of my neck with a claim of his own.

If I'd been full of warmth before, now I was blazing. Even getting intimate with *one* guy I actually desired was a pretty new thing, and to be nestled between two, caressed and adored with every movement of their hands and mouths—it was so much I could barely focus on my thoughts, but it was *good*. So good.

I wanted both of these men, and they both wanted me, and maybe there wasn't anything so complicated about that after all.

The two of them seemed to have come to the same conclusion. Emeric sank onto the couch next to me, pulling off his gloves and then tucking my legs over his lap to make room, his mouth never leaving mine. I kissed him back, one hand delving into his thick hair while the other reached back to trail along Noah's jaw. The scion nibbled a path up the side of my neck that left me gasping into Emeric's mouth.

When I eased back to kiss Noah on the lips, Emeric ducked his head to nip my earlobe. Noah's hand kept stroking up and down my outer thigh, Emeric tucked his arm around my waist, and I felt perfectly cocooned in heat and pleasure.

We stayed like that for longer than I could keep track of, one and then the other guy reclaiming my mouth, their hands teasing across my body but never venturing anywhere too intimate. As if we were feeling each other out, the three of us together, figuring out exactly what kind of balance we could strike before we risked tipping it by trying more.

Emeric kissed the nape of my neck in just the right spot to provoke a jolt of bliss. I whimpered low in my throat and turned yet again to seek out his lips with mine, but he stopped me before our mouths met, his fingers drawing a giddy line over the skin just above the collar of my shirt.

His voice came out low and a little hoarse. "You have no idea how badly I want to make this what that afternoon in Portland should have been."

The afternoon when we'd almost slept together. An answering clang of desire reverberated through my body.

I glanced back at Noah to gauge his reaction, however well he could put together the pieces from what Emeric had said and the brief mentions I'd made of our truncated relationship. The scion's hand stilled on my thigh. "Whatever you want, *ma belle*," he said. "You're in the driver's seat."

Suddenly that felt like an immense responsibility. What if we went too fast and ended up crashing and burning?

But... part of me wanted to try in spite of that fear.

We didn't have to go all the way. I could put a stop to

things the moment any of us seemed uncomfortable. Right now, I was the one in control.

I set my hand over Noah's, twining my fingers with his, and returned my attention to Emeric. "We can take this to my bedroom and… see where it goes."

The hunger that flared in his gaze nearly incinerated me in the best possible way. He took my other hand, and I stood up still enclosed between them. When I stepped toward my bedroom door, they came with me.

Faced with the bed, a swell of uncertainty gripped me. The guys waited on either side of me, giving me time to work out how I'd like this to go.

Their patience reassured me. I was ready for this. I wanted to embrace everything they could offer.

I tugged my shirt off over my head. Emeric sucked in a breath and grazed a finger over my shoulder blade along my bra strap. Noah cupped my jaw and kissed me, and we moved as one body onto the bed.

What happened next was a blur of kisses and caresses and clothes yanked off. The guys conjured heady delight everywhere they touched, and between the two of them, they touched *everywhere*. I arched into them, gasping and growling and finally moaning as Emeric worked my nipple over with his tongue at the same time as Noah swiveled his thumb over my clit. Desire burned through my body, demanding satisfaction.

I rolled onto my back and glanced at Noah one more time to check his expression. He nodded, smiling at me so fondly my chest threatened to explode with love. He kissed my cheek, his hand rising to stroke my breasts, and I pulled Emeric over me.

Emeric settled between my legs, his eyes wide and searingly bright. When I gripped his erection, he groaned. Then he tucked his hand against my slit and murmured the protection spell, his gaze never leaving mine for a second.

My core throbbed for him. I raised my knees, and he slid into me just the way I needed it.

My head pressed back into the pillow, my hips canting upward. Noah kept summoning fresh waves of pleasure with his fingers skimming over my chest and his mouth scorching my shoulder and neck. Emeric thrust in a steady, building rhythm, his breath already fragmenting. He braced his titanium arm beside me, and I grasped it, knowing the squeeze of my fingers would travel through the metal to his nerves.

I wanted him as he was, broken and put back together, just like me if more visibly.

I swayed to meet him, lifting to receive his kiss and then seeking out Noah's mouth. The pleasure inside me surged higher and faster than I'd ever felt it before. Clutching both of them, I let the wave sweep me over the edge.

Emeric's hips jerked as he followed me. His head bowed. "Fuck, Cressida, you're so— I've never—"

When he couldn't seem to gather his words, I simply stroked the side of his face, high on the rush of my orgasm. He looked down at me, somehow still shocked to find himself here but with a smile he couldn't restrain. I glanced over at Noah with a smile of my own that was a promise of things to come later, and he grinned back at me, rakishly disheveled. I'd made a mess of his ponytail.

The guys considered each other for a brief, slightly awkward moment. Then Emeric withdrew, lying down at my other side, and a weird sense of peace settled over the three of us.

Maybe this arrangement we'd only just forged would still go to hell once the reality had more time to sink in. But for now… for now I had no complaints at all.

It wasn't anywhere near nighttime, but I let my eyelids drift shut just for a moment. There was nothing else we *needed* to do. I'd like to linger here in this contentment for as long as I could.

At least, that's how I felt for a few moments. After a minute, a strange restlessness gripped me. I tried to ignore it, but it wriggled through my limbs with the growing sense that there was something very important I needed to accomplish.

Frowning, I pushed myself upright and reached for my nearest pieces of clothing. Noah propped himself up on his elbow to watch me, his expression puzzled. "Are you all right, Cressida?"

"Yes," I said, because I was, wasn't I? I just— "I need to talk to Rory." No, that wasn't quite right. "I need to talk to all of the barons."

Emeric sat up, his brow furrowing. "Why? Are they even here right now?"

The question provoked a tremor of assurance through me. I found myself nodding. "All of them." I tugged on my panties. "I'll text Rory. I'm sure—"

"What do you need to talk to them about?" Noah interrupted, pushing himself upright too. He looked even more confused than before.

"I—" I didn't know. It was important, but—why didn't I know?

I paused with my jeans balled between my hands, trying to force some awareness to the surface—and a jab of pain shot through my gums. I pressed my hand to my cheek over the offending tooth.

Emeric leaned toward me. "What's going on, Cressida?"

"I don't know," I admitted. "I—I need to talk to the barons. I'm not sure why. And my tooth is hurting—I'm sure it'll be fine."

"Your tooth," he repeated, and his face blanched. He shot forward as I moved to slip off the bed, his hand closing around my wrist. His voice came out with a detached note as if he was repeating something he'd heard before. "No one looks too closely in the mouth."

"What are you talking about?" I jerked at my arm, but he held on firmly. More pain radiated from my tooth. "Emeric, let me go!"

"No." He stared at me with an expression so haunted that it stopped me in my tracks. "*Why* do you need to see the barons, Cressida?"

"What does it matter?" I demanded, but my heart was suddenly thumping fast. Noah eased closer to us, his gaze darting between us.

Emeric swallowed audibly. "It matters because I

overheard the reapers talking the day they brought you in. They were supposed to be discussing what they were going to do with you, but I assumed they'd moved on to another subject. Something about some kind of spell they were going to unleash on the barons from within the wards."

He paused, and his voice turned ragged. "But that could have been the same subject after all. I told you they've made a pet project of perfecting latent magic… I think their spell to destroy the barons might be inside *you*."

ABOUT THE AUTHOR

Eva Chase lives in Canada with her family. She loves stories both swoony and supernatural, and strong women and the men who appreciate them. Along with the Royals of Villain Academy series, she is the author of the Flirting with Monsters series, the Moriarty's Men series, the Looking-Glass Curse trilogy, the Their Dark Valkyrie series, the Witch's Consorts series, the Dragon Shifter's Mates series, the Demons of Fame Romance series, the Legends Reborn trilogy, and the Alpha Project Psychic Romance series.

Connect with Eva online:
www.evachase.com
eva@evachase.com